The Mystery of Misty

Carol Kopec

Royal Fireworks Press

Unionville, New York
Toronto, Ontario

This book was written remembering the first pekins, Prince Charles, Queenie, and Angelica, and the three little girls who loved them, Aimee, Rachel and Anna

Author's Note:

Some of the places in this story really do—or did—exist. Others are places I made up. Boiling Springs kids could tell you which are which. All the characters, though, are purely fictional—except for Lipper, the friendliest chicken I ever knew.

Royal Fireworks Press
First Avenue, POB 399
Unionville, NY 10988-0399
(914) 726-4444
FAX: (914) 726-3824
EMAIL: rfpress@ny.frontiercomm.net

Royal Fireworks Press
78 Biddeford Avenue
Downsview, Ontario
M3H 1K4 Canada
FAX: (416) 633-3010

ISBN: 0-88092-406-3   Paperback

Printed in the United States of America using vegetable-based inks on acid-free recycled paper by the Royal Fireworks Printing Co. of Unionville, New York.

CHAPTER ONE

BAD NEWS

It was ten minutes past 9:00 on an early June morning—hardly the time to expect visitors. Nick had gathered eggs earlier—there were six today—and Dad had just finished bringing them to the table, scrambled and sunny. That's when they heard the hum of a motor and the crunch of gravel on the drive.

"Maybe someone wants to fish the pond!" Nick said hopefully, glancing into the hall toward his bamboo pole.

"Not likely," said Winnie, who was sitting with a view right through the dining-room door and out the kitchen window. "Not unless fishermen are wearing lavender suits and black high heels these days."

Lucy had to lean over and across the dining-room table to get a good view. What she saw was a lady with a sharp nose and flat brown hair pulled back from her face with a headband. She was carrying a briefcase and marching toward the back door.

"Who do you suppose it is?" she asked, turning to her parents. But they didn't hear. They were still at their end of the table, heads close together, whispering.

Dad got up. "Listen, would you kids mind excusing Mother and me for just a few minutes? We hadn't expected Mrs. Strope so early. Here Lucy," he said, handing her the toast they'd barely begun eating. "Why don't you treat Sapphire this morning?"

Mother was scurrying about, opening drawers, handing Winnie scissors, handing Winnie a vase. "...irises—and some of those lovely pink sweet william," they heard her

1

say, just before they were all whisked out one door, and the mysterious visitor was invited through another.

In just seconds the three children found themselves outside the front door, blinking and squinting in the morning sunshine.

"What do you suppose that was all about?" Winnie asked. "And who's this Mrs. Strope?"

"I don't know," Lucy answered, "but if I lived to be a hundred, I never thought I'd see the day when Dad would give me toast for Sapphire!"

They laughed. Lucy was always sneaking treats to her pet. But when Dad caught her, she'd get the same old lecture: white pekin ducks could forage perfectly well for worms and snails and plants, and their grocery bills were high enough without adding gourmet snacks for animals.

As if the pekin knew they were discussing her, she began squawking loudly, somewhere by the creek.

"There she is." Nick pointed. Sapphire had just stepped out of the water in the shallow place under the sycamore and had started toward them. Half way up the hill she stopped, eyeing Winnie suspiciously, then Nick.

"She sure is shy," Winnie teased. "Just like you."

Lucy glared at her older sister.

"OK, OK, squirt," Winnie said gently, taking two pieces of toast out of Lucy's hand. "I'm starved," she explained, seeing Lucy frown.

"Me too," said Nick, taking some for himself. "I can't believe they wouldn't even let us finish breakfast. I wonder what they're talking about."

"Look," Winnie said, "you guys feed the duck, I'll get the flowers, and we'll meet back here in five minutes. Then we can listen by the living room window. OK?"

"Uh-uh. I'm going now," said Nick. He was already running.

When Winnie had gone too, Lucy walked down to meet Sapphire, offering her the remaining toast. The small duck ate greedily. Lucy smiled as her fingers skimmed her pet's silky white feathers—then the blue ones on her wings. In the morning sun, those twin patches looked the color of real sapphires. Oren McCaleb at the hatchery said the blue meant Sapphire was special, that she had a streak of wild duck in her.

"You are special," Lucy said, remembering, "and it has nothing to do with your ancestors."

As if she understood, Sapphire snuggled contentedly in Lucy's arms. But only for a second. Winnie was back in no time, her vase full of long-stemmed irises. Two especially dark ones were leaning into her hair, making her look like an island girl or some red-haired hula dancer.

"C'mon," she repeated impatiently. "I'm going to put these down by the front door. I'll meet you by the window."

But when they got there Nick was nowhere in sight. "No wonder," Winnie said, cupping her hands over the glass. "No one's in there. Let's try the kitchen."

But no one was there either. Or in the dining room. Mystified, they continued on around the house and had come nearly full circle when they caught sight of a pant leg and one blue tennis shoe dangling from a low branch of the beech tree.

"What on earth..." Winnie began, but Nick gave a loud "Shh-sh" and pointed upward.

There they were. Upstairs! All three of them, staring out of Mom and Dad's bedroom window.

3

"What in the world are they doing up there?" Lucy whispered as the girls ducked behind a screen of blackberry bushes.

"Maybe she's a painter too," Winnie suggested. "Maybe she wanted to see how Mom got that angle on her barn painting—the one she won the prize for."

Lucy doubted it. Whenever other painters were around, Mother smiled and laughed and talked a mile a minute. Now her whole body was stiff and half-turned away from the visitor. And she kept biting her lip, which she practically never did except when she was trying to keep from crying.

"Or she might be one of Dad's friends—a new professor maybe, and he's showing her a view of the countryside."

"I don't think so," Lucy answered. "Summer school doesn't even start till next week, so why would she be all dressed up and carrying a brief case on her vacation?"

The longer Lucy looked at them the uneasier she felt. Mom always joked that she had ESP with animals. Right now she wished she had some with people. She wanted to know why Mom looked so miserable.

"I wish she'd go home," Winnie said forcefully. "Then maybe Mom and Dad will tell us what's going on."

As if she'd been talking to a genie, the three figures turned away from the window. In just minutes, they were walking out the back door.

Nick jumped down from the tree. "They've been through every room of the house!" he exclaimed quietly. "Even the bathrooms!"

The three of them exchanged puzzled glances. Mrs. Strope was looking all around, praising the "beautiful grounds," when she noticed them. So Dad called them over for introductions. It almost didn't seem necessary.

"Why you're the little redhead that danced in the Nutcracker last winter, aren't you? You were wonderful!"

Winnie blushed and smiled and didn't look at all like the person who just wished Mrs. Strope would go home.

She knew Nick too. "Fastest 10-year-old in the county," she exclaimed in that loud, nasal voice. "My son Joe runs too, so I saw you at the last meet. Congratulations on your 100-yard dash."

"Gee, thanks," said Nick, grinning, scratching into his sandy-colored hair. Then he asked what school Joe went to, how he did at the meet.

When Dad introduced Lucy, Mrs. Strope just stared.

"Lucy's our animal lover," Mom helped. "Someday you may be taking your pets to a veterinarian named Lucy Peterson!"

Lucy smiled, glad her Mom had thought that up. Now she was off the hook. Mrs. Strope's eyes had turned away from her, onto her long, white car.

She looked back before getting in. "I'll be in Williams Grove anyway today, so I can stop by for a signature and be back on Monday with a sign."

"What sign?"

"What's going on in Williams Grove?"

"Why does she need a signature?"

Everyone seemed to be talking at once as they walked back inside. Instead of heading them back to eat, Mom pointed to the living room, which was enough to replace all their loud questions with an expectant hush. She motioned them to the couch and sat down opposite them, on the edge of the rocker. Dad stayed standing, right beside her.

"About three weeks ago we got a call from our landlady, Mrs. Rummel."

"Williams Grove!" Lucy interrupted. "Mrs. Rummel lives in Williams Grove doesn't she?" It was the rent checks that reminded her. She'd biked to the post office lots of times to mail them.

"Is she the one Mrs. Strope is going to see?" Nick asked.

"Oh no!" Winnie piped in. "Mrs. Rummel isn't going to sell our house, is she?"

Mother swallowed hard. "I'm afraid so. I'm afraid she is."

Lucy's heart gave a little jump inside her. She glanced at Nick. He looked shocked too. "You mean Mrs. Strope is going to buy our house?" her brother asked.

"No. Mrs. Strope is a real estate agent. She's going to try to sell it," Dad explained. "Of course, Mrs. Rummel feels badly about this. When she called she offered us first chance as buyers. But her asking price is way more than we can afford. So now she's working with Strope Realty."

Mom's eyes looked a little watery. Lucy just stared. Nick said not to worry, that they'd find another place just as nice.

"Do you think you kids could be happy living in a neighborhood again?" she asked hopefully.

Nick just looked at her, his eyes growing wider every second. His voice came out in a kind of croak. "But what about my chickens?"

"That's right! Sapphire! I can't leave Sapphire," Lucy thought to herself. Her heart was beating faster now. Her thoughts were racing. You weren't allowed to keep ducks in the city. And Sapphire was too shy to let anyone else take care of her.

"Why couldn't we find another country place—like this?" she asked.

"We've already tried," Dad answered, "but with Harrisburg so close, not to mention Philadelphia and DC, those city folks looking for summer homes have driven prices right through the roof. Even for rentals. You know, kids," Dad added, "those new townhouses in Mount Holly will be opening soon. It's not the country, I know, but they're being built around a huge common green. And Molly Pitcher Park would be practically next door. Or maybe we could find a small house in Carlisle."

Lucy couldn't believe her ears. Mount Holly was nice, sure. Carlisle was nice. But not if you had a pet duck that you loved as much as anyone in the world. Not if you had chickens.

Nick was on his feet now, fists clenched, face as red as after a track meet. "I can't give up my chickens," he said. "Dad. I can't."

"There are a lot of friendly farmers around here who would be glad to take care of those chickens—and let you come visit too," Dad said softly.

But Nick wasn't listening. He was turning. Running. Lucy heard the back door slam.

"What about Sapphire?" Lucy asked. Her voice was so loud she surprised even herself. "Nobody around here likes duck eggs. Here all people want ducks for is to eat."

"Lucy, Lucy," said Dad, shaking his head and coming closer. "Mother and I have discussed this. Sapphire is almost wild. She's never even learned to sleep in a pen. She spends all her time alone, near the water. The only person she'll come to is you."

"She's not afraid of Nick," Lucy answered weakly.

7

"Only if he's with you," Dad answered. "Look, Lucy, you know it: Sapphire is too shy to make a good pet. But she's just fine here. Hasn't she done just fine, foraging for snails and worms and plants? Oren McCaleb says this kind of duck in this kind of countryside could find most of her own food. And the village duck pond isn't that far. The ducks are fed there all year long. We could take the canoe and let Sapphire follow us out there. Show her the way. Then if she ever got hungry she'd know where to go."

Tears were welling up in Lucy's eyes. But she was eleven already. She wasn't going to cry. She wasn't. "I'll find Nick." The words came out high and squeaky. Then the tears spilled over. Then she ran.

Dad had no idea how much she fed Sapphire. How much she'd always fed her. Sapphire expected it now. And even if she could learn to find her own food, to live on bugs and worms, she'd never understand. What would she think when Lucy just disappeared one day? Lucy was her only friend in all the world. Sapphire didn't even trust other ducks.

This must be what it's like when someone you love dies, Lucy thought darkly as she opened the door to the shed. Nick was where she thought he'd be, sitting on the roosting bars. He was holding Marshmallow.

Lucy sat down beside him, and Lipper flew onto her arm.

"Poor Lips," Lucy thought out loud. It wasn't going to be easy for her, either.

Lipper was Nick's friendliest chicken. She'd had her beak clipped at the hatchery when she was a baby—like all the other chicks. But she must have squiggled or jumped when it was her turn, because they took practically all of

8

it off and it never grew back. Her beak looked like lips, and she couldn't peck right, so everyone made a fuss over her and fed her by hand when they thought of it. Lipper was spoiled and very tame and always landed on people like they were bushes or roosting poles.

"Who's gonna like her?" Nick asked bitterly. "To us she's great—but other people always think she's obnoxious. Especially grownups. Especially when she lands on them, and they have nice clothes on."

They both laughed. Then it was quiet, and it all seemed more terrible than ever.

"Nobody could ever love them the way I do."

"At least you'll be able to have somebody take care of them," Lucy answered. "I'm supposed to just leave Sapphire. Just leave her to take care of herself."

"Oh, Lu." Nick was surprised. "I'm sorry," he added, putting Marshmallow down. "Lucy, there must be something we can do to stop them. There must be."

"Sure. Like find enough money to buy our house? How are kids supposed to do that? Look, Nick, we've got to be realistic. We've got to find somebody good to take care of the chickens." She paused, thinking. "Maybe Toby Neely's folks would take them. You go there all the time anyway. And Toby loves chickens."

When Lucy left the shed, she knew Nick would be all right. He was already thinking. Making a plan. But Lucy couldn't do that. She really didn't know what would happen to her pet.

She headed for the water, for Sapphire, past the house, past the walnut tree where the grass was getting high, tickling her legs. There was a smell of wild rose in the air, blowing all along the hill down toward the creek. At the bottom she stopped and sat down, leaning against the sycamore that dipped its patchy bark into the water. She couldn't see Sapphire. But in a minute Sapphire would see her. And come.

And then she was there, her bill on Lucy's neck, lifting her dark hair, then waddling around, nosing in her pockets.

"Oh, Saph, not any more," she said. "Not ever anymore. You've got to learn to take care of yourself now." And the thought of disappointing her duck, of coming to her empty-handed tomorrow and the next day and the day after—the thought of Sapphire alone, without a friend in all the world, was more than she could bear. She put her arms around her duck, laid her head on the soft, white feathers, and cried and cried.

"Whoever comes here," she thought to herself, "just has to love you, Saph. They just have to."

CHAPTER TWO

WORSE

Mrs. Strope did come back on Monday, with a large red and white FOR SALE sign which she pounded into the top of the drive. After that she came around a lot, bringing people to see the house. She bragged about it as if it were her own and worth a million dollars and not just a crumbling, drafty old farmhouse. Some people, Lucy learned, liked old houses—the older the better. And theirs was two hundred years old, so that made it pretty good.

It was on Friday of that week that she brought Ellen and George Barngrover, from Newville. Lucy followed them everywhere and got up enough courage to ask if they liked ducks. When they said yes, she asked if they wanted to see Sapphire, and even though Mrs. Strope frowned hard at her, she took them down by the creek. Nick came too. And the chickens. That turned out to be a mistake, because Ellen's short, fluffy hair looked for all the world just like a nest and when she sat down Lipper flew right onto it, making her scream and jump and run in circles on the lawn. Mom and Dad heard from the house and came running. Mrs. Strope got red and scowled at them ferociously. So Mother said absolutely and positively from now on to keep themselves and their pets out of sight and not to bother anyone.

So Nick and Lucy took to using Dad's bird-watching binoculars and hiding in the main attic where they'd listen through the floor. Nick and she would tip-toe around in the dark, following the voices and footsteps underneath them, then discuss whether or not they'd make good duck-keepers. If the people wanted to see the attic, they'd hide in the old green army trunk. It was safe because the hinges were off, but it was a tight squeeze and very hot. Luckily no one stayed up there for long.

By the middle of July the phone wasn't ringing so much. "She's asking too much for the house," Dad said one night at supper.

"Does that mean our house might not sell at all?" Lucy asked hopefully.

"Well," Dad replied, "I wouldn't get my hopes too high. Mrs. Strope has decided to place ads in the big city newspapers. Who knows? Some millionaire from New Jersey might decide this place is just his cup of tea."

Lucy couldn't imagine that a millionaire would want their plain old house. So she hoped like anything Mrs. Rummel would keep her price high and that no one would buy it for a long, long time. Or ever. But she knew she couldn't take chances—not with Sapphire.

So she and Nick went down to the creek every day. There was a place there where the water curved around and got shallow and the earth poked up in spots. It was private because the vines and willow branches made curtains and pretty too because of the way the sun filtered through the green, making streaks and spots of light that would dance over the mud and water when the wind blew.

Every afternoon they'd poke there in the shallows, finding worms or little beetles for Lucy's duck. At first they fed her out of their hands. Then they taught her how to dig, planting worms on the muddy bank and calling her over and pointing. They always rewarded her with hugs and praise. And Nick's giggle. He thought Saph's front nose dive and simultaneous back wiggle were hilarious.

One afternoon in late July they had barely started this routine when Nick put his trowel down and stood back up facing the house. Then Lucy heard it too—the low sound of crunching gravel. Someone was pulling into the driveway.

When they came out from under the willows, the children saw a long, shiny black car. It stopped just under the beech tree. For a few minutes nothing moved except the dappled sunlight playing over its roof. Then a man in a grey uniform got out and opened the back door. Out came a slender lady wearing a rose-colored suit and dark glasses. In the sun her long hair looked gold and shimmery. As she pushed it back from her face, they could see sparkles on her fingers. The man who came out after her was much older. They could tell by the hunched look of his shoulders and his getting-stout middle. His hair was silvery grey. He put one hand on the lady's shoulder, and they both stood still, heads back, staring up at the house. The door on the other side opened. Straight brown hair with a white headband popped up, like a bubble. It was, unmistakably, Mrs. Strope.

"Mom didn't say we were going to have anyone today," Nick said in a puzzled voice.

"Maybe they arranged this one in a hurry," Lucy suggested. Or maybe, she thought to herself, Mom didn't want to spoil their day. These two certainly looked like they could afford the place. "C'mon," she said out loud, "we've got to get to the attic before they do."

They raced for the front door. Going in they heard Mrs. Strope's nasal laugh, a fluttery laugh in answer, and a deep voice saying something about putting a tennis court where the meadow garden was.

Lucy slowed on the attic stairs. The air felt like a furnace, and it was hard to breathe. She waited at the top while her eyes grew accustomed to the dimness. At first all she could see were straws of diamond over her head

13

where the roof was pieced together. Then the dark separated into silhouettes of black on grey, and then into shapes with dusky colors.

To one side, just beneath the sloping roof, she could make out her parents' old packing boxes and the new ones filled with winter clothing. Far ahead of her she could see the other pile of belongings, the ones that were here when they came: the Rummels' things. Mom and Dad's orders were never to touch them. Which wasn't hard. They were just cartons filled with magazines and old wallpaper, a mailbox with RUMMEL painted on it, an old lamp. The only really interesting thing was the bed—a beautiful tall-postered bed, in pieces now against the wall. Lucy liked the birds that flew around inside the carved panels on the old headboard. She liked to imagine how it would look put together, how it would feel to sleep in such a fancy bed. And looking at it didn't hurt anything.

"They're coming up!" Nick whispered. Lucy jumped. He'd climbed up behind her so quietly that he'd startled her. "Their license plate says New York. Did you hear about the tennis court? He wants to put a tennis court where the garden is!"

Before Lucy could even nod in answer, they heard footsteps in the hall below and stood alert, waiting.

"Graydon, look. You can see the kitchen through this grate in the floor. Look at the design. Whatever is it for?"

The voice was coming from Mom's bedroom. They tiptoed quickly to the east wall and bent down, heads toward the floor.

"This, Julia," he answered, "is how they used to heat these bedrooms. Hot air rises, you see, and so they'd cut holes in their ceilings to pass heat up to the second story.

14

This grate is a kind of souvenir from the past. Quaint," he added.

"City slickers!" Nick whispered to the floor. Then he looked up at Lucy. "Quaint," he whispered, nose in the air, one hand pressed back against his forehead.

He looked so silly Lucy almost laughed out loud. But Nick was just acting smart. They didn't know what the circles were for either when they'd first moved in two years ago. And this hot air business was something they'd never have figured out for themselves. It was freezing upstairs in winter.

Downstairs Mrs. Strope was clearing her throat. "Well, actually, Mr. and Mrs. Dourman, it's not exactly just a souvenir. The oil furnace heats the first floor beautifully. But...well, there are no direct connections to the second floor. So... uh, well, you might say these vents are still functional, although, of course, it still stays rather cool up here in the winter months."

"Are you saying there's no heat up here?" the lady asked. "How barbaric!" There was a silence, then the lady spoke again. "Well, Graydon, we would just be using it for the summer months. Still, it's incredible people still live like this."

Nick rolled his eyes. Lucy felt angry. She wondered where Mother was. If she'd heard.

"Oh, darling, let's have a look at that charming little room that faces the stream."

That was Lucy's room. Nick put his hand on her sleeve as they tiptoed over. "They're not even going to live here in the winter. That's no help to Sapphire!"

As if she didn't realize. Winter was the very hardest time for animals to find food.

"This would make a lovely nursery or child's room," Mrs. Strope said. She always said that—every single time. It was because Lucy's room was the smallest. But Lucy didn't care that it wasn't big. Her window faced the huge, old walnut tree and the hill that was covered with daffodils in Spring and tiger lilies in Summer. Farther on was the stream. She could hear it running quietly on summer nights when the window was open. Besides, the smaller attic was right next door and up a step, and that was like having another room—a secret room.

"Fortunately we needn't worry about children," Julia Dourman said quickly. Then: "This room would be wonderful as a studio, don't you think, Graydon? We could knock out this wall and use that attic space too. Put in a few skylights. Yes, painted white it would be splendid."

"Splendid," agreed Graydon.

"Splendid, my foot," Lucy thought. she felt like she was going to throw up. "I've heard enough," she whispered to Nick. "Listen for me, OK?"

Back outside, Lucy found a place near the driveway where she wouldn't be seen, behind the wild rose bushes, close to the compost pile. She wrapped her arms around her legs and rested her head on her knees. The ground here was damp, and the air, so close to the compost, smelled rich and earthy. She thought of the garden. She wondered how it would smell when it was covered with cement. She thought of her room, turned to white space, as if some witch had waved a magic wand making every good thing disappear. She thought of Sapphire. Of course they wouldn't love her. Who was she trying to kid?

Sapphire. She must have sensed Lucy was out, thinking of her.

16

"Quah-wah-wah-wah-wah." The quacking was coming closer. There she was. She was coming to Lucy. Crossing the driveway.

And then Julia and Graydon Dourman were at the back door.

"Well, look, Julia darling," the man said, waving his hand, "beautiful wildlife, right at our doorstep."

Julia flicked her head, pushing her long blonde hair from her eyes. Rainbow colors sparked from her fingers. "Graydon," she said flatly, "my sister Althea had ducks when she was small—Snowball and Goldie." They both laughed, as if the names were hilariously funny, then stopped quite as suddenly as they'd begun. "Ducks," she began again in that light but sharp voice, "are the world's messiest creatures. And the last thing I'd want on my doorstep. Besides," she added, "that quacking is so obnoxious." And she walked right past Sapphire in her rose-colored shoes toward the shiny car.

♋   ♋   ♋

Dad took forever getting home that night. He'd taken his ecology class to the experimental farm at Emmaus. Mother said that because of the weather he was probably driving the day students right to their homes instead of dropping everyone off at the college.

By 6:30 the whole countryside looked eerily dark. Wind was whipping the trees around and large rain drops were beginning to splatter on the back flagstone walk.

"Just in time," he said exuberantly as he walked in. His cheeks were red and his dark hair a little wild-looking from the wind. He held up a large bag. "Strawberries," he announced, although he didn't have to. The whole room smelled suddenly like a berry patch.

"It's a new kind of everbearer. Imagine. Berries all summer. And they're big," he added, opening the bag and holding it out to Lucy. "Like bowling balls." But Lucy didn't laugh, and she didn't take one, though she managed a smile.

Her dad looked at her thoughtfully, then looked at her sister and brother, and then at Mom. "So what's up?"

At supper, over mashed potatoes, pork chops, and creamed cucumbers, he listened to the whole story. Lucy didn't have to do as much talking as she thought she would. It looked like everyone felt the way she did.

"She called us barbarians!" Nick said angrily.

"She thought my wallpaper was 'ghastly,'" Winnie said, pursing her lips, flicking back her copper-colored curls. This didn't quite work with Winnie's hair, which was thick and flicked right back with a mind of its own. But the meaning of the imitation was clear. Winnie was furious because she'd spent months redoing her room and had chosen the paper herself.

Mother just looked at Dad and said quietly, "I think this house was meant for a family, Spence. I don't think there'll be much laughter or warmth inside these walls after the Dourmans have moved in."

So Mom was thinking it, too. They probably would move in. There was no reason why they couldn't. Lucy stared at the mashed potatoes on her plate, at her fork, crisscrossing them, making tic-tac-toe patterns on the flattening white mound. The wind that had been murmuring beneath the table conversation was growing louder, more violent. She glanced up at her Mom and Dad, at the ferns behind them on the deep window ledges. She let her eyes wander up the window glass.

The hanging lamp with its candle-like lights was mirrored there, and farther down the backs of her parents' heads, a carrot-colored oval and a thick shock of black, still messy from the wind. In between she could see her own heart-shaped face, her dark, curly hair, pulled back today in a pony tail. She stared, and her own dark eyes stared back at her.

"I wonder how Mrs. Rummel would feel about her garden being turned to concrete?" Winnie was saying.

And then a terrible crash of thunder and lightning happened all at once. And the lights went out.

In the window the reflections vanished. And there, standing just yards away, out in the open wind and seeming to look straight at Lucy, was a mysterious-looking yet very beautiful duck.

CHAPTER THREE

I'VE COME TO HELP YOU

Lucy had never seen a duck like it. Never. And ducks were everywhere in Boiling Springs, all along the shiny ribbon of the Yellow Breeches Creek—not just white pekins like Sapphire, but rubbery-faced Muscovies, fat, waddly Aylesburies, and wild mallards too.

Surely she would remember if she'd seen one like this before. He had a copper-colored head, wing feathers dark as smoke—and an astonishing bill. In that flash of lightning, it had been a pale, eerie blue, just the color of sky on a day when the moon stays out. Yet that blue bill wasn't what surprised Lucy most. It was the look he'd given her.

Unafraid of the lightning and wind, as unfluttered by the storm as a ghost, he seemed to be staring straight at Lucy. And like one of those trees outside swelling with wind, Lucy's mind opened and swirled dizzily with a crazy thought: "Come out," he seemed to be saying. "I need to talk to you."

Lucy couldn't leave supper, of course, and run out into a storm. And she couldn't bring herself to tell her family. Not even Nick. Instead, after Dad had found matches and candles, she finished her supper quietly and went up to her room and waited by the window. How did the duck know whose window to turn to? Yet there he was, looking straight at her again, as if he were saying: "I'm waiting."

When the storm was finally over, Lucy slipped on her rubber boots and her old green sweater. She grabbed a trowel and bucket, so she wouldn't look suspicious. Nick and she often dug for nightcrawlers after a rain like this, putting a sign in the driveway later to bring in customers.

Outside the air was cool and damp. The little wind that was left made Lucy shiver. When the duck saw her coming he began walking too, only away from her, toward the creek. He turned back every now and then, as if to make sure she were following.

It occurred to Lucy he was taking the road you couldn't see anymore, the one that used to come around in front of the house. She'd learned about it from Mrs. Strope, who was explaining to some clients one day why the back door was near the highway and the front door faced away from it, toward the Yellow Breeches. That surely must have been long ago, thought Lucy, looking at the tall maples and beeches pushing up from muddy earth where carriages used to travel.

The duck finally stopped down at the creek, next to the sycamore. The closer Lucy got, the prettier he looked. His red head had the same glisteny quality as bubbles, only its color was that of fire. His beak glowed bright blue, as if still carrying the light of day.

When she got almost within reaching distance, she stopped short. She blinked her eyes. She rubbed them. He seemed to be... shimmering, or something. Waving. As if he were hot air over an August sidewalk. But no. It must have been a trick of the dusky light, or a last spray from the wet leaves, for as she stepped even closer his form seemed to solidify; he looked as real as anyone.

Cautiously she crouched down and touched him. He wasn't at all spooked. Instead of flapping his wings and flying off—like another duck might—he welcomed her with a raucous, high-pitched quack so airy-sounding that it made her laugh. But only for a second, for suddenly she seemed to be sensing something again. What he wanted her to understand.

A gust of wind filled up the sycamore. A shiver went down her back. "Listen to me"—that was the meaning. "Believe in me. I've come to help you." Then he turned around, toward the water, leaving Lucy to blink and swallow and wonder if she were going crazy.

She turned toward the creek too now, looked out at the water. In the still, shallow part, the leaves were still dripping rain, filling the water with rings, shining circles. They looked like coins, Lucy thought.

She reached out a hand to stroke the strange duck. Her hand touched wet grass. She looked down. There was nothing there. Not on this side. Not on the other. Only sodden lawn and two fat pink worms who'd come up to enjoy the weather.

Where had he gone? She'd only looked away for a second. Had there been enough time for him to walk away? She didn't think so. And if he'd flown, she would have heard his wings flapping. As close as she was, she would have felt his wings flapping.

Just then Sapphire appeared, waddling up from the shallows. Her heart went tight when her little duck practically dived right into her green sweater, still remembering the days of bread in her pockets.

"Oh, Saph," she said. "I don't do that anymore, remember? Then thinking of the worms, she pointed to the grass, even picked one up for her pet. While Saph was eating, she walked through the bushes, up toward the road and down again. But there was no sign of the blue-billed duck. He'd disappeared as quickly as he'd come. As if he really were a ghost. Or a magical being.

The air was still, but she shivered again anyway, remembering those rainbow colors, how he'd vanished, and most of all, those strange wordless messages she'd felt so sure of. He'd come to help! But no. That couldn't be. He wasn't a goose that laid golden eggs. And she wasn't living inside a fairy tale. Magic was just a story they told. To kids.

Get a hold of yourself, she thought sensibly. You're just frantic about the Dourmans, that's all. You're letting your imagination run away with you. Sure, animals can tell you things without talking—things like 'I'm starving' or 'Come play with me' or 'You're wonderful.' But they do not say things like "I've come to help you." Or "Trust me." You must have imagined it.

Sapphire was back now, rubbing her legs like a cat.

"But I wish there were such a thing as magic," she told her duck as she bent down and held her arms out. "I wish there were a magic that would let me keep you," she whispered as the small duck nuzzled into her neck, into the thick curls of her pony tail. A lump rose in her throat. How could she leave Sapphire with those Dourmans? How could she?

"Did you hear them today, Sapphire?" she asked, stroking the duck's small head. "Did you understand?" She held Sapphire close, thinking, wishing there were some way to change things. Nick had said there must be a way, but she hadn't listened. Maybe she should have thought harder. Maybe she should think harder now. The air grew slowly colder. It was getting quite dark. She'd have to go in.

On the way up the hill she walked slowly, staring at her red boots, which looked purply grey in the darkness. Right. Left. Her feet sank into the wet grass, making tiny bubbles squidge up around the edges. She wished, oh how she wished she could figure out some way to change things.

She tried to think about the situation logically, but she was tired, and it was just images that spun through her head. Mrs. Dourman's light hair, flashing rings, her cold eyes on Sapphire. Nick's hand on her arm in the attic. The storm. The flash of lightning, the strange, blue-billed duck, Winnie saying softly, "What would Mrs. Rummel say?"

Lucy stopped. "What would Mrs. Rummel say?" Winnie asked again, inside Lucy's head.

Well, what would she say? Lucy asked herself. She looked up at the sky, where a great racing cloud was blowing the moon like a bubble.

"That's it!" Lucy said out loud, to the sky, and began racing up the hill toward the house.

CHAPTER FOUR

LOCKED OUT, LOCKED IN

"Nick, will you come with me to Mrs. Rummel's?" Lucy was out of breath, her heart still pounding from the race up the hill.

Nick was stacking baseball cards along the edge of his bed. He looked up in surprise. "Are you crazy?" he asked. "Mom would go through the roof if she found out. Where've you been anyway?" he added, glancing down at her boots.

Lucy ignored the question, pulling the chair away from the desk and sitting down to face him. "Mom doesn't have to know. We can skip swim class Wednesday morning and be back before her painting class is over. Say yes, Nick. I need you. You know how to talk to grownups."

Nick just looked at her. "If Mom found out..." He started shaking his head. "We'd get grounded sure. And the Dillsburg Devils game is coming up..."

"Nick! Remember, there must be something we can do...? Remember your chickens? And you're not even gonna be in the South Middleton League if we have to move this summer."

Nick looked away, silently staring at Ernie Banks while a flush spread over his freckled cheeks. "You're right," he whispered. Then he looked back and grinned.

On Tuesday night they decided to tell Winnie about their plan—just in case something went wrong. Funny, she didn't yell. Or call them nutty little kids. She just looked thoughtful for a minute, then said, "Well, I think Mrs. Rummel should know those Dourmans are total creeps.

And I hope your plan works." Then her blue eyes got wide, and she grinned. "Joe could give you a ride home from Williams Grove, I bet." She got up and ran out to the hall phone.

Nick rolled his eyes. "Oh brother, she thinks of more reasons to call him up. But I never thought we'd be a reason." They both laughed, hands over their mouths, so Winnie couldn't hear.

Joe was sixteen and Winnie's latest boyfriend. His dad owned Bixler's, the village store, where they sold hand-dipped ice cream cones and fishermen's extra fish, and on Wednesdays, pastry from O'Gorman's Goody Shop in Williams Grove. It was Joe's job to go get it and also to pick up fruit and vegetables from local farmers.

Winnie came back humming, her cheeks a bright pink. "Can you meet him in front of O'Gorman's at 11:30? It'll save you the whole way back. You probably won't even be late for lunch."

If Lucy and Nick looked nervous the next morning, Mom was much too absent-minded to notice. She was running late, too busy for breakfast and pulling easels up from the cellar when they said good-bye. "Be good," she called after them. "Have fun!"

Winnie came out at the very last minute, just as she and Nick were climbing onto their bikes at the top of the drive. Her feet were bare, and she was still in her robe. "Be careful. Don't you take a ride from anyone but Joe. And watch out for traffic. Oh," she added, as if remembering something important. She raised one hand in the air, fingers crossed. "Good luck."

26

Their biggest worry at first was seeing other swimmers, but all they saw on Creek Road was the Mayberrys' cow, who mooed loudly as they passed. The village square was deserted too—just a few mothers watching their children down where the creek slowed and spread out and really did look like a pond. The clock tower in front of the tavern said 8:55.

Once they passed the summer resort of Allenberry, they breathed a little easier. Or Lucy did. Nick had been riding no hands, off and on, and whistling. Now Lucy relaxed too.

The Yellow Breeches sped along beside them, sun-glittered and mostly empty, except for two girls in a canoe, who waved when they went by, and a fisherman in waders. Then they turned away from the water, and all they could see were cornstalks. Then they were bouncing over the railroad tracks at Brandstville. Then they were there.

They stopped at the Grove pharmacy to cool off with soda and ask for directions. That's when they got their first wind of trouble.

Two men were sitting at the soda fountain looking at the Grove Gazette.

"Jes' look at that Rummel House," the older one said, sadly shaking his bald head. "Sprayed the sidewalks, the stone walls, even part of the fence with that damn orange paint. No way you can get that stuff off."

"Teenagers!" snarled the other. "Oughta be horse-whipped, if you ask me."

"Excuse me, sir," Nick piped in. "We couldn't help but overhear. Has something happened at Mrs. Rummel's place? We were just on our way there."

The younger man put his coffee cup down and swirled around on his stool to face them. "Old lady went into the hospital for an operation. While she was gone some young vandals used her place for a party. Damn near ruined it too."

Lucy became so panicked she jumped right into the conversation. "You mean Mrs. Rummel's in the hospital?"

"Yah. She's at St. Patrick's," the bald one said.

"No. No," interrupted the other. "She's back home now. Since yesterday. Her sister's come down from Scranton to stay with her. That old Elva Schrader now," he chuckled, "she'll keep those darned kids away. I heard that if kids get within ten feet of the house she comes out with a broom to chase them away."

Lucy must have looked terrified to hear it, because they both laughed and the old man added. "Now don't be lettin' Jake here scare ya. As long as you know her I'm sure Elva won't be rude."

"Well, we don't exactly know her," Nick said.

"But she's our landlady," Lucy added quickly, seeing the man frown. "Our mom needs us to talk to her. Can you tell us where Barner's Hill is?"

The hill was filled with mansions. The higher they climbed, the fancier they got. Lucy was encouraged. If Mrs. Rummel was this rich, she certainly didn't need to sell their house in a hurry. She could wait for a family of duck-lovers. Kids. And once she knew about Sapphire, she surely would.

But when they got to the hilltop they turned to each other in surprise. Mrs. Rummel's house was big, sure, but it looked more like a friendly, run-down farmhouse than a mansion.

"What's that house doing here?" Nick asked.

28

"I know," Lucy agreed. "It'd look more at home on Creek Road. In the middle of a cornfield. With the Mayberrys' cow out in front."

One thing about it though was just what they expected. The ledgestone wall, the iron-spoked fence that sat above it, even the sidewalk had been sprayed with bright orange paint. Someone had tried to wash it away but you could still see two big B's that must have said Brandtsville Bears. Just underneath them you could still make out "Class of..."

"Well, you sure can't blame that Elva person for being suspicious of kids now," Nick said, his blue sneakers straddling an orange streak on the sidewalk. But Nick wasn't really thinking of the paint. He was eyeing the gate. And so was Lucy. Her guess was that ordinarily it had simply swung open for visitors because the chain lock on it looked new. How were they supposed to get past that? How did anyone know when to come?

"Look, there's a bell!" Lucy said, pointing to the top of the gate post. She went over to it and reached up. "Well, OK," she said, taking a deep breath. "If she comes out with her broom we'll just tell her who we are and why we came..."

"Yah—and what if she asks our names and phone numbers so she can double check with our parents?"

Lucy hesitated, her heart pounding, staring toward the house. Then she rang the bell anyway, taking courage from the house itself. It looked so friendly—the bird bath to one side, the cheery geraniums by the front door, the ruffled curtains inside the front window. The front window! Lucy drew a sharp breath, and her heart beat even faster. A face was next to those curtains—an old and wrinkled face, framed in wild hair flying like white flame, with eyes narrow as the slits in a coin bank. Her mouth was set in a tight line.

29

"Oh, no!" Lucy said. "She sees us, and she looks mean!"

Within seconds the front door flew open, and Lucy stepped back. She did it without thinking, then quickly caught herself, remembering Sapphire. She smiled weakly, but the old lady never smiled back, just kept charging forward, her back straight as a rod, her black skirt flapping around her like bat wings. Her arms were in the air. Her hands were fists.

"Can't you kids leave poor Hannah in peace? First them devils. Now you littler ones come to gawk." She was at the gate now. "I'll give you ten seconds to leave this property. Then I'm calling the police. Do you understand? Do you?" With this she bent her head toward the gate, her sharp nose almost poking through. Her finger was pointed at Lucy.

"Please, ma'm. We didn't come to see the paint. We didn't even know it happened. We came to talk to Mrs. Rummel. We have to..."

But the lady had already turned and was racing back to the house, probably to the telephone. She hadn't heard a word Lucy said.

"If she calls the police, they'll ask our names, you know," said Nick, already walking his bike toward the street. "They'll call Mom sure."

Lucy stood still, panicked. They'd come all this way....

The air was still and hot. Lucy heard the whistle of a cardinal and a far-away voice, another voice, a door slamming. She ran after Nick and grabbed his arm. "Someone's in the yard," she whispered. "Let's park our bikes down by that brick house with all the pine trees. Then we can have a look out back. No one will see us over the ledge if we stoop.

"Lucy!" Nick cried. "I'm telling you. We're going to get into trouble."

"We're in trouble already," Lucy whispered. And so's Sapphire. Not to mention your chickens. C'mon, Nick. We can't give up now." She was surprised at her own insistence. Her knees were shaking. "I just want to look out back. That's all."

There were lots of trees: oaks, gingko, pawpaw. But there was sun in the yard too. A garden full of daisies sat in one bright spot, the patio in another, its latticed roof casting patterned shadows on the white table and chairs below. To the side of that and down the slope a ways a reclining lawn chair was tucked into the shadows of an old beech. Someone was in it.

"Maybe it's her!" Lucy whispered. She was on tiptoe, staring through the spokes that rose above the ledgestone wall. "Boost me, will you?"

Nick stared at her in amazement. "You can't go in there!"

"Oh, c'mon, Nick. Go back to the gate and ring the bell. You can run away fast. She'll never even see who did it. But it'll give me time to get into the yard."

"And what if Mrs. Rummel's as mean as her sister?"

"Then I'll run away," she said flatly. "C'mon. Lift me up."

Once onto the low cross bars she sprang over easily. Now she would wait. She glanced up again at the garden, the quiet patio, the faraway figure in the chair. Next to it she saw something she hadn't noticed before. Its ears were high, its teeth clenched. It gave a low growl. It sprang toward her.

31

CHAPTER FIVE

HE'D JUST VANISH

It was too late to climb the fence again. Anyway, that would only make the dog attack for sure. So Lucy did what she was taught to do in such a situation. She crouched down and placed her right hand out, palm down, to show she wanted to make friends. Then she did something she wasn't taught to do but always did anyway. She thought at him. Hard.

"How strong and fast you are. How beautiful. Will you be my friend? My name is Lucy. Please don't hurt me. Please."

Black as thunder, the doberman raced toward her, his bark rising into the canopy of trees, ringing down again like curtains around Lucy's ears. She shut her eyes. And then all was still. When she opened them again he was standing in front of her, his head cocked to one side, as if curious to know why she wasn't running away. Lucy smiled, noticing how shiny his coat was, how the brown mark between his eyes looked like the letter "S." She felt he was listening to her thoughts. She hoped he was. He sniffed her hand. She touched his silky neck.

"Blackie! Blackie!" said a tired-sounding voice from above, on the hill. "What are you doing there? A rabbit again? Leave the poor bunnies alone. Come, now. Come, boy. Come."

Lucy followed Blackie back. His tail wagged, and he looked back at her and then at the old lady in the chair as if to say, "Look at the bunny I caught today."

Lucy knew she'd have to talk very fast or she'd be shooed away again by the fast-moving, suspicious sister.

"Please, ma'm, are you Mrs. Rummel? I have to talk to you about something. It's very important. The most important thing in the whole world." She'd barely gotten her name out when the straight-backed lady came charging through the back door, hand on her hips. Her voice was loud and harsh: "I thought I told you kids..."

"Please, Elva, it's all right. This is Lucy Peterson. She's—I think—the daughter of Spencer and Lee, who rent the farmhouse?"

Lucy nodded, surprised she knew.

"Lucy, this is my sister, Elva Schrader, come all the way from Scranton to help me out for a bit." Turning to Elva she added: "I've invited her for lemonade, Elva. Could you get some? Some sugar cookies too, if it wouldn't be too much trouble."

"Hannah Rummel, you're really too tired for company, and you know it." She glared—first at her sister, then at Lucy. Then she turned and stomped off.

"She's not really so bad-tempered," Mrs. Rummel said. Then she laughed. "Well, not usually. She's just upset over this foolish vandalism and my being sick."

Mrs. Rummel didn't look sick, just tired. She was pretty, in an old-person kind of way. Her hair was wispy and purest white and lifted away from her face like the clouds off hills on windy days. Her eyes were a light, clear blue—just the color of Nick's best puries. Where was Nick anyway? Did he get away in time?

She turned, looked down the hill, and spotted his red baseball cap on the other side of the fence. Mrs. Rummel turned too, following Lucy's gaze.

"That's my brother Nick. He just rang the bell again so I could come over the back way."

Mrs. Rummel's shoulders and chest shook with laughter. "Such excitement in my life. For years no one comes to see me. Now visitors are everywhere—like ants. Go. Go get your brother. I'll hold Blackie."

Mrs. Rummel wouldn't let them say anything until Elva had come with the lemonade, and they'd settled themselves into the shade. But Lucy couldn't drink, and she didn't want to sit. She just stood on the grass, gripping the cold glass tightly. Then she blurted out her speech—or the parts she remembered. By now it was all jumbled, but she did say about the Dourmans and how they were nasty and only summer people and about poor Sapphire.

When she finished there was silence. You could hear bees buzzing in the nearby daisies and Mrs. Schrader inside, shutting a cupboard, walking briskly across the floor.

Mrs. Rummel had been listening with her eyes closed. Now they were open. They looked a little watery.

"I'm sorry," she said slowly. "If there were anything in this world I could do to help you, I would do it. I swear it. But look. Look at me," she said, patting the bony bumps of knees under her faded robe. "I move like a turtle on these legs now. And even turtles don't need walkers," she said with a scowl, waving one hand at the piece of flashing metal beside her chair.

"Do you see? Elva can only stay a few weeks. Then I have to hire a nurse. And the money runs, flies away. The bills! So many bills! If I don't sell the farmhouse soon, they'll take this house, this place where I've always lived, where my Johnny grew up, where Otto and I were young together."

Lucy stared at her cookie, at the sparkling sugar crystals. Her mind was sparking too. Why couldn't Mrs. Rummel's Johnny help out?. At least till they found some other buyers. She wished it wouldn't be impolite to ask.

"What about Johnny?" Nick piped in. "He's your son, right? Couldn't he loan you some money?"

Lucy felt a sweep of gratitude for her brother's bad manners.

"Oh no. He mustn't know," Mrs. Rummel replied. "Already he says the house is too much for me. That I should sell it. Come to Wyoming, where my bones wouldn't ache so. But, children, this is my home. I belong here. I love this place just like you love your duck and chickens."

Well, Lucy thought. She swallowed over a lump in her throat and tried to blink the tears away.

"I know, I know," Mrs. Rummel said, gently reaching out a hand and patting Lucy's arm. Then she sighed. "If only there were some way to help," she whispered. "Why you of all people ought to be living in that house. My grandmother's ghost is telling me so. Whispering it in my ear. This very minute."

Nick dropped his cookie. He didn't look down for it either. He was too busy staring at Mrs. Rummel's ears. Lucy was too. But they didn't see anything. Just two tiny gold earrings in the shape of a cross.

"How did your grandmother get to be a ghost?" asked Nick, the ghost-story fan. "Does she haunt your house?"

"And why did you say your grandmother wanted me to live in the house?" asked Lucy, surprised at being singled out.

Mrs. Rummels's earrings glittered and shook as the old lady laughed. "Young man," she finally said, "she haunts

35

your house, if she haunts anyone's. She was born in your farmhouse. Died there too. But I didn't mean my Gram was really a ghost—just that my memory of her makes me know what she would want. How strange," she added, as if to herself, shaking her head.

Lucy wondered what was so strange. She settled herself finally onto the cool grass and waited for the old lady to go on.

Finally Mrs. Rummel looked in her direction, but her eyes seemed unfocused, a little dreamy. "My grandmother's name was Lucy, too, you see." She smiled. "Lucy Sarah Silverling. And just like you she loved ducks. As a matter of fact she collected them. She had dozens."

"She did?" Lucy asked, surprised. What kind?"

"Oh, many, many kinds. She collected odd ones. Her parents' friends would bring her ducks with fancy markings. Her aunts and uncles even brought sea duck eggs—all the way from Baltimore and Boston—and she would hatch them under her banty hen. Everyone called her the duck girl." At this Mrs. Rummel chuckled, shaking her head from side to side.

"It's hard to imagine my grandmother a duck girl—or any girl at all. To me she was just a kindly old white-haired woman, thin as a broom, with large dark eyes. When I stayed with her, she always had calico cats, a collie, and a pond full of plain white pekins. But in her stories of when she was little! She told me she'd had polka-dotted ducks, ducks with heads that seemed to wear fluffy hats, ducks that could weed the garden or count to ten or even give wishes! When I was little, I believed every word, of course. Now I have to stop and think, try to sort out what she really had from what she just made up. Now I know crested ducks have fluffy heads. And I've heard of geese that eat weeds. But I never did know of any waterfowl that could count to ten, did you? And as for giving wishes, well, let's just say Grandmother had a vivid imagination. And who wouldn't in her situation? She needed one to survive."

Mrs. Rummel stopped, held out her glass and asked Nick to pour a bit more.

"Why did she need one?" Nick asked as he tipped the green pitcher.

Mrs. Rummel took another sip before she spoke again. "She wasn't lucky. Not like you and me, anyway. She had no sister. No brother. In 1860 there was no plate glass factory on your road, no dried milk plant, no neighbors at all. For miles and miles around it was utterly wild. She was alone. There was just Lucy and her ducks.

"They were her only friends. And maybe when they couldn't do the things real children do, she'd pretend they could. Or maybe, just to amuse herself, she'd pretend they could do other things. Amazing and interesting things. Who knows? Who knows what those ducks could really do?" She stopped for a second, finished up her drink, then looked at them both. "Her favorite duck, I remember, was called Bluebill."

Lucy's heart gave a jump. "Bluebill?" she croaked. Nick looked over at her curiously. She cleared her throat, as if it were a cookie and not pure shock that had lodged there. "Did he have a blue bill?"

"Well, it's what Gran said. Should I believe it? I did when I was little. Should I believe he could vanish, like a ghost? Ghost, you see, is what Gram almost named him, because he would disappear so fast she'd never see him go. She said she never even found where he slept, for he'd just vanish when she was penning in the others. And should I believe he could read her mind? She said he did. That he could hear her no matter how far away he was. That he could hear her even if she only called him inside her mind. Now should I believe that?

"Lucy's face was burning. Her head spinning. But she had the presence of mind to answer Mrs. Rummel's question. "Sometimes I think Sapphire hears me when I call her in my mind—or when I'm thinking of her."

"Yeah! It's ESP!" Nick said with a grin. "Lucy's good at it too!" He started telling how Lucy had found Lips once when she was lost, just trying to tune in to her. But Lucy wasn't paying attention. She kept thinking of the Bluebill she'd seen. And how he'd vanished.

Mrs. Rummel chuckled as if Nick's story were a made-up joke. But she didn't say she didn't believe him. She only said: "You two do have a lot in common with my grandma. I think she would like you very much. As I do."

Leaving Mrs. Rummel's was a lot easier than getting in had been. It was slower though. Mrs. Rummel really did move like a turtle. Nick and Lucy put their glasses in the sink while Elva settled Mrs. Rummel onto the living room couch with her knitting. Then they said goodbye, promised they'd come back again to visit, and walked out the front door.

Half way down the sidewalk Lucy slowed. Hesitated.

"I'll be right back," she said, then turned and ran back up the walk. She knocked once, to be polite, but opened the door herself so as not to bring old Mrs. Schrader back.

"Mrs. Rummel," she asked, did your Gran ever tell you what color the rest of Bluebill was?"

Mrs. Rummel looked up with a curious expression. "Lucy, it's too bad you couldn't really meet my Gran—the both of you with your ducks!" She put her needles and yarn down then and stared hard at nothing in particular, as if she were seeing some image from the past. "I do remember, for Grandma always talked about that Bluebill. He was dark, like smoke, and his eyes were golden, and his head I especially remember, because Gran always used to say it was just the color of Elva's."

Mrs. Schrader had come into the room at the sound of voices and Lucy looked at her now. "Was it white then?"

Both old ladies burst into laughter. Lucy stared, astounded, as straight-backed Mrs. Schrader bent over and slapped her knee. "Dear child," she finally said, "I wasn't always sixty-eight, you know."

Mrs. Rummel wiped a tear from the corner of her eyes and after one last giggle she added: "When Elva was younger she was the beauty of Cumberland County. It was her hair, Lucy. Thick and curly—like yours—and the most beautiful shade of coppery red you've ever seen!"

CHAPTER SIX

MISTY--SHORT FOR MYSTERY

The ride back to town was fast and quiet. Nick rode head down, no tricks, his green Schwinn traveling straight as an arrow down the bumpy brick sidewalk. Lucy knew what he was thinking: Good-bye house. Good-bye Sapphire. Good-bye chickens.

At Main Street they turned right and headed for O'Gorman's. They could have found it blindfolded just by following their noses that morning. The smell of fresh bread filled the air, making Lucy feel hungry, but her watch said it wasn't lunchtime yet. They were on time.

They waited on the hot curb, scraping their shoes over street stones. Lucy stared down at her right thong, at the side strap that was dangling by a thin string of rubber. But she wasn't thinking about shoes, and neither was Nick.

"What we ought to have," said Nick, "is one of those ducks Mrs. Rummel's grandma had. The one that gave wishes. Or maybe that Bluebill. Maybe it could make other things disappear beside itself. Maybe it could make our house disappear—when the Dourmans come back." He giggled at his own joke. He laughed. He took his baseball cap off and slapped it on his knee.

"Maybe we do have Bluebill."

Nick stopped laughing. "What are you talking about?"

"You remember when I asked you to come with me? The night of the storm?"

"How could I forget?" he answered. "I had to play ball the next day with boot prints all over my shirt. What were you doing outside that night anyway?"

So she told him. Everything. "He had a blue bill, Nick, just like the other Lucy's duck. And when I went back in there this morning—Mrs. Rummel said the whole rest of him was the same too—gold eyes, red head, grey body. Everything. And that's not all."

Nick just stared, waiting.

"He seemed to be... telling me something."

"Like ESP?"

"I don't know. I guess. But it wasn't like knowing where Sapphire might be or that the chickens want some treats. It was like ... real thoughts. Like..." she hesitated, and then just blurted it out, "I've come to help you."

She held her breath.

Nick kept staring. Did he think she was totally flipping out? That she'd gone crazy worrying over Sapphire? That she'd been in the sun too long? Nick had never doubted her before. Not about something important.

He opened his mouth, but just then an engine roared around the corner. Rock music filled the air. Brakes squealed. Then Joe was in front of them, grinning down from the high cab of his dad's pickup. "Hi little Lou! Nick-o. Ready to go?"

After settling their bikes in between bushels of snap beans, tomatoes and melons, Joe said he'd be back in a flash and headed for the glass-doored entrance.

Nick climbed into the cab and Lucy followed. The vinyl was so hot it hurt her legs. She scooched up, turning to her still-silent brother.

"Geez, Luce, he finally complained. "I can't believe all this happened, and you didn't tell me."

Lucy let out a breath she didn't even know she was holding. "I'm sorry, Nick," she began. "I don't know exactly why..." but Nick was already talking.

"I never heard of an animal ghost. But why couldn't there be animal ghosts? Could you see through him? How did he disappear? Was it like in the movies? You know, poof!"

"No. No. It wasn't like that at all. He just looked like a duck. I mean, for a minute he looked a little...wavery or something, but I think it was just the rain. I never saw him go." She frowned. "And I'm not totally sure about the message..."

Before she could say more, Joe popped his head in the window, throwing a half dozen bags of bread at Nick and setting a box of lemon tarts in her lap. Then he was in the other side, starting the engine and turning the radio as far up as it would go. Then it was too late and too loud for more talking—about anything.

⊙   ⊙   ⊙

When they walked in, Mom was stirring a big pitcher of iced tea. Platters of ham and tomatoes and bread were already on the dining-room table and a big vase of black-eyed Susans.

"Who's coming over?" Lucy asked, glad they wouldn't have to scrounge for lunch, as usual.

"No one," Mom answered. "I just felt like doing something nice, that's all."

Lucy guessed the drop-in art class must have gone great. There'd sure been lots of students anyway, judging by the paintings drying against the washer and dryer, the cupboards, the back wall. Nick was studying one, which was unusual. It was Lucy who always looked them over and talked to Mom about them.

"These are kind of wild," Lucy commented, glancing from the shed, done in very wobbly line, to the creek with little blue stars floating on it, to the meadow, mounding toward the top of its canvas, leaving only a thin blue streak of sky.

"I was trying to loosen the students up today," Mom replied. "I told them to try to paint what they felt, more than what they saw."

"Harriet Walsh's technique is really improving, don't you think?" Mom asked, pointing to a messy rendering of the chickens. "Nick, have you seen this one?"

But Nick was still by the back window, looking at the painting under the sill. Lucy came over. Her heart popped right up to her mouth. Her already hot face went hotter.

The three of them stood there and looked at it. It was a blue-billed duck standing on the hill above the creek. Ever so delicately, the artist had sketched in the grass behind him. A leafy branch. A moss covered rock. He was completely transparent.

"That's Lila Roberts'. She does great work, doesn't she? Aren't you going to tell me about your swim class?" Mom called out from the back door. But they were already gone.

They looked everywhere along the hill above the creek, even along the steepest parts, even up along the highway.

"Rats!" Nick muttered under his breath, as he heard Dad's car pull into the driveway.

Just as they were starting back toward the house, something made Lucy turn around. And there he was, half way up the smooth stretch of hill, as if he'd materialized, as if he'd just been beamed down.

43

Nick stood stock still, staring up at the tall beech tree, the sky, the insides of the flowering rose just yards away from the blue-billed duck. "Where'd he fly down from?"

Then suddenly Lucy wasn't looking at the duck; she was staring at the grass around him. She moved swiftly in spite of Nick's whispered, "Go slow! You'll spook him!"

She bent down. She reached for the shining gold coins sharply outlined on the brilliant grass. She reached. She blinked. Dappled sunlight moved over her hands. Her fingers touched only grass.

"What are you doing?" Nick asked.

"I...I thought I saw money..."

She looked at the duck. The eye that faced her was also round and gold. And intelligent. He was thinking at her..

"You'll need money if you're going to stay here..."

Lucy stepped back in surprise, and though the August sun was warm on her skin she got goosebumps on her arm. And then she wondered, "Did he really say that—or did I just imagine it?"

Just then Nick touched the head of the duck, who squawked in alarm and backed away, toward Lucy. "This duck's real!"

Lucy looked at her brother's surprise. Had he expected his hand to pass right through that red head? Hadn't she told him she'd touched this duck? She touched him now, gently, looked at him. But no thought came. Had she imagined it? Had she?

Then Dad was there, briefcase in hand, squinting up at them. "What this? A redhead? Wow! I haven't seen one of those in a while."

Nick and Lucy looked at each other, then at Dad.

"You mean there's lots of ducks that look like this?" Nick asked. He sounded disappointed.

Dad laughed. "He does look odd, doesn't he? But so do all his brothers and sister and cousins. I wonder what he's doing here. This time of year you usually only see redheads up north—in the Dakotas, on up into Canada. Though I've heard a few breed up by Lake Eerie. Still, that's a long way from Boiling Springs."

"Geez, I thought he was a real mystery duck..." Nick began.

Dad just stood there, staring, scrunching up his forehead.

"He is a mystery," Lucy said stubbornly, though suddenly she wasn't so sure.

Dad just kept staring, then finally said, "You're right, Lucy. Look at him. He's in the wrong place. He's even in the wrong time."

"Wrong time?" Lucy and Nick asked at once.

"He's wearing fall plumage already. Besides, he's supposed to be wild. He's acting like a pet." He chuckled. "You're something else, Lucy. You could probably tame a tiger. Have you named him yet?"

"Let's call him Misty!" Nick suggested. "Short for mystery!"

Dad said: "Wait till I tell Oren McCaleb about this one."

At lunch Nick talked a mile a minute, telling Mom about the redhead who'd flown off course and molted in the middle of summer, and how they were going to ask Oren McCaleb, and how they were going to call him Misty, short for Mystery. Listening to him, Lucy could tell he didn't think Misty was really a mystery. Not like before. Not like a mystery that talked—and could help them. Just to

45

prove it, he passed her the ham plate, and added: "Hey, Luce, maybe Misty and Sapphire could be friends. Then if we move...

"We're not going to move," Lucy said loudly, dropping the plate. Nick stopped talking as the plate rattled, the fork banged, and the room sunk into silence.

"Now Lucy," Dad began quietly, "we are going to move. We've explained that to you. And...well...as a matter of fact, it's probably going to happen soon. The Dourmans are sending in a real estate inspector from New York—a Mr. Wickfield. He'll be here tomorrow. If the house looks OK, they'll probably make an offer."

Lucy just sat there, stunned. Dad was still talking but his voice seemed like it was coming from beneath water...

"...time we got Sapphire to the village pond...make sure she knows where to go if she's hungry..."

It can't be true, Lucy thought, her heart beating like a drum. It had all seemed so far away before!

Now they were making arrangements. Dad was busy with exams. Would Winnie take the kids...

And now Winnie was looking straight at her. "...in half an hour. OK?"

"Huh? OK," she heard herself say. She picked up her ham sandwich. She put it down again. Suddenly she wasn't hungry.

CHAPTER SEVEN

PECKING ORDER

"All right," said Winnie. "Get in. Let's get this show on the road."

Nick turned back to Lucy and rolled his eyes. They were the ones who had got the canoe down. They were the ones who found the missing oar in the pile of scrap lumber. They were the ones who had waited twenty minutes while Winnie french-braided her red hair and changed barrettes three times.

Lucy smiled, still a little halfheartedly. She poked Nick with her banana. "Get in, slowpoke." Then she turned to make sure Sapphire was still there.

"Are you sure you don't want a rope around her or something? Are you sure she'll follow?"

Lucy looked down at her banana, the loaf of white bread, the grapes. "Winnie. She'll follow."

As if to prove it, Sapphire stretched her neck toward Lucy's full hands, squawking loudly. Lucy slipped her a grape.

Winnie and Nick took the oars. Lucy sat in back so she could call to Sapphire and coax her with food. She didn't want to give too much away at first. Sapphire had to associate food with the duck pond, not the boat. And she wanted her to be hungry when they got there.

After lunch Lucy had thought it over. How important this trip was. She couldn't depend on miracles or magic to save Sapphire. She had to depend on the real chance she had—the chance to teach Sapphire how not to starve when they were gone. That was what was most important.

And who knows? Maybe the Dourmans would change their minds. It was possible, wasn't it?

Lucy held onto that thought as the canoe slipped down the green-lit creek. If she held on to it tight enough, she could almost enjoy this trip. How nice to be able to give Sapphire presents, after all this time. Her duck swam after them, dipping her head sometimes, arching her neck every now and then and squawking at Lucy, begging for grapes as though it were a game.

Up front Winnie was giving orders. "Left. Faster, Nick. OK. Watch those rocks. It's shallow toward the right."

After they'd gone around the first two curves, Winnie sighed. The creek would be deep and fairly straight now, until they were almost there.

"Well, what did Mrs. Rummel say this morning?" she finally asked.

"She's poorer than we are and needs money—fast," Nick answered.

"She says she doesn't have time to wait for anyone better," Lucy added. "She was nice, though."

"How depressing!" Winnie said. "And that real estate inspector's coming tomorrow. Imagine. The Dourmans sure don't waste any time."

Lucy listened. Her stomach was starting to feel queasy again. Sapphire was behind them, happily unaware of what any of this meant. In the sun, her feathers looked as white as snow on a bright day and you could see her orange feet paddling just beneath the clear surface. Every once in a while, the sun shone down, just so, and she looked like she was swimming through puddles of diamonds.

"Mom said the whole thing is very suspicious."

"Suspicious?" echoed Nick.

Lucy turned around.

"Yes. Very. Mr. Wickfield doesn't want anyone around when he comes. He didn't say so, of course. He just said things like he'd want to come when they'd be at work or had other plans, because he didn't want to inconvenience them, and he knew how irritating it was to have someone poking around while they were eating or watching TV. Mom thought he sounded like a burglar, so she asked for references. He gave her his business number, and said she could check it, and he said he'd have the Dourmans call right back. Which they did. I answered the phone myself. Still, doesn't it seem funny to you?"

"I guess," said Lucy, not seeing why he'd want to be alone if he weren't a burglar. And if he were a burglar, they'd know exactly what he looked like after tomorrow, because they'd have to let him in. That would make him a very dumb burglar. She turned away again. The last thing she needed now was something else to worry about.

Sapphire had stopped near a murky side puddle. Lucy called out and threw another grape, but the little duck didn't completely catch up until they'd banked just at the edge of the park.

Winnie stared down into the wavering water, pushing back the curly wisps that had slipped out of her braid. "I'm going to stop in at Betsy Drexel's." She looked up at Lucy. "Unless you need me..."

"We're OK."

"Meet you here in about an hour then."

"Right," said Lucy walking backward already, waving her sister away, then quickly glancing around for Nick, who'd already disappeared. Luckily, Sapphire was still in the water. The trick would be getting her to stay there.

There were a lot of mallards just ahead, and it would be just like shy Sapphire to jump out at the sight of a crowd.

"Lucy dear! How are you, child?" It was Mrs. Trostle, sitting on a park bench, waving a lace-edged hanky. Her other hand was on Nick's arms. So that's where he'd gone.

"Lucy. Come. I want you to meet my daughter."

Lucy looked at the plump, middle-aged lady sitting next to her.

"Lucy, this is my daughter Emmy. Emmy, this is Lucy—one of my Sunday-school students."

"How do you do, uh..." Lucy began.

The lady laughed. "Mom, she can't very well call me Emmy. I'm Mrs. Evans," she said kindly. "And I'm delighted to meet you. Oh and Lucy, this is Bear."

"He's beautiful!" Lucy exclaimed, petting the huge Irish setter at her feet. The dog licked her, then nosed into her bread bag. Just then Lucy had an idea. "Could I...I mean, would you like me to walk him for you?"

"Sure, Lucy, you can take him for a walk if you like. Just don't go any farther than the clock tower, OK?"

"I'll keep my eye on her," said Nick, backing out of Mrs. Trostle's grip.

As soon as they were out of earshot, Nick turned to Lucy. "What are you doing with this dog?"

"I'm keeping Sapphire in the water," whispered Lucy, her eyes on the creek, following her duck.

"Oh," said Nick smiling. "That's smart."

Lucy smiled back.

There were always a lot of people at the square—fishermen from out of state, people stopping after a meal at the tavern, or a trip to the bank or post office. With school out now, there were lots of kids too, but Lucy could only see two with food. Just ahead of them a fair, curly-haired boy was throwing handfuls of popcorn at two hens and a drake. Farther on was a little girl with straight black hair and missing front teeth. The rest of the ducks were there, clamoring around her. Lucy glanced at Sapphire, wondering if she saw her too. Sure enough, Sapphire's eyes were on her and on the light dusted crumbs falling from her hands like confetti.

Sapphire swam; Lucy walked in closer.

"Great luck," Lucy said. "Old powdered-sugar doughnuts. Sapphire's favorite."

Lucy asked Nick to take the dog, clutched her own food sack even tighter, and moved up the bank slowly, to get a better view. Would her duck join the others?

Sapphire swam very slowly, staring hard, as if amazed to know she wasn't the only hungry duck in the world. She passed the three popcorn eaters with a shy, almost whispered quacking and headed for the spot where the little girl was standing, stopping just behind three pekins who formed a bright white spot in the circle of darker mallards.

"Look, Mommy, look!" the little girl cried. "See the pretty white one with blue on her wings?"

Lucy's heart swelled. She glanced back at Nick, to see if he'd heard. He grinned back at her.

The little girl threw a bit of the sweet sugary bread way out in the water, so Sapphire could reach. But just as Sapphire was about to grab it, the white duck in front of her turned and pushed her away, taking the prize in his own bill. The little girl tried again and the circle of birds rearranged itself. It was like watching a kaleidoscope, seeing the bright pieces change places, making a new design. Now there was a large, chocolate-colored drake next to Sapphire, who butted her sharply, taking the crumb for himself.

The little girl tried a third time, and already Sapphire was arching her neck, squawking. It was as if she knew it was hers and was telling everyone. "Good for you," thought Lucy. But just as Sapphire was about to take it, the drake came darting toward her. Lucy's heart skipped a beat. The big duck was angry, and judging from the way the other ducks moved to one side, she realized he must be a very important duck. He poked Sapphire with his bill, the crumb forgotten.

"You'd better swim away now, Sapphire," Lucy thought at her. "Swim away. He's the boss and that's just how it is. It's called pecking order, dummy. You don't have a choice."

But Sapphire stayed. Why didn't she move? Didn't ducks know about dominance by instinct? Did they have to grow up in a flock to know? Was she frozen with fright?

"Move Sapphire!" This time Lucy's voice came out loud. But it didn't do any good. Sapphire didn't budge. And this made the big duck furious.

He reared up in the water, spreading his dark wings to slap her. Sapphire squawked wildly and began to swim away now—fast. But not fast enough for the drake, who came after her, skimming the top of the water like a bullet, his neck low and straight and hard. His bill reached for Sapphire's soft feathers. He jabbed at her, again and again. Sapphire swam faster, in a frenzy, first moving to one side of the stream, then the other, zigzagging crookedly, awkwardly away from her attacker.

For just a second everything seemed to stop. Voices died away. Running children were suddenly still. Everyone's eyes were on the water, and the only living things in motion were the ducks swimming away, fast as speedboats. And then Sapphire was just a small dot of white, bobbing on the silvery thread of faraway stream and the drake was coming back, head high, triumphant. It was over.

"He's mean," the little girl told her mother.

"It seems like it," said the woman, "but that's just how ducks are. Someone is always bossing someone else around. Next time throw lots and lots of pieces at once. Then the big drake will be too busy eating to notice what the little ones are doing."

"That's what I should have done," thought Lucy, running back up the stream, trying to spot Sapphire again. "Why didn't I remember about pecking order. I knew about it. I could have thrown the whole bag of bread at that stupid drake."

"Sapphire! Sapphire, come back!" Lucy called. She was already at the Motters and then onto other neat lawns, over flower beds, then smack up against someone's chain-link fence. She'd have to get her feet wet to go around it. And Sapphire was still racing away in panic, swimming with all her strength towards home.

Lucy knew Sapphire could hear her. But the duck didn't even turn around to look. She'd probably never come back. Not for grapes. Not for bananas. Not for anything. She'd stay at home, where she felt safe. "But dear, dumb Sapphire," she thought, "your home isn't going to be safe anymore. That's what you don't know. And how am I ever going to make you understand?"

It was midnight. Lucy was still up. For hours she'd lain awake, listening to the soft murmurs of the creek, guilt lapping like water at the edges of her mind. She blamed herself over and over for not counting on Sapphire's being pushed out, for not throwing twenty pieces of bread in all directions, for not figuring it all out ahead of time.

Sapphire was up too. She'd been squawking and fussing at the water's edge, swimming in circles, every since they'd gotten home. Over and over Lucy got up to make sure it wasn't a fox or the Mayberrys' dog. But she never saw anything more than Sapphire in the moonlight, swimming in circles, remembering the day.

Nick was up too. Ever, ever so faintly Lucy could hear him through the wall, pacing, which is what he did when he was worrying, thinking, or dreaming up plans. At half past midnight, the footsteps changed direction. They headed toward her door.

She heard a rap. "Lucy are you up?" she heard him whisper. "I've got an idea."

CHAPTER EIGHT

A PLAN

The next morning they biked over to Byers Lumber. Nick brought four quarters he had left from cutting grass, but he didn't think they'd need them. "I think woodshavings and sawdust are free," he told Lucy as they walked under the GIGANTIC SALE banner. "Anyway, we don't need much. Termites don't leave mountains of it around you know."

Lucy followed her brother past the electric fixtures, the nail bins, the garden supplies, all the while wishing her thong strap hadn't broken. Her old tennis shoes were hot and already too small. The right one was rubbing at the back of her heel. She frowned down at those stupid shoes as she passed the sprinklers and bumped right into the back of Nick, who'd finally found a clerk. It was Ned Hollenbaugh, his Little League coach.

"Watcha building today, Nick-o?"

Lucy waited for Nick to explain. She might have known he could never just stick to sawdust. First it was the league championships, then the prospects for Marshmallow or one of the other chickens to win a ribbon at the county fair, and then his two latest knock-knock jokes. He finally mentioned about a little bit of sawdust, but the little part didn't register with Mr. Hollenbaugh. He must have still been thinking about Marshmallow, because when he walked into the back room he hollered at the boy back there: "Give these kids some sawdust. They've got a chicken coop at home." Before Nick could protest, Ned was going on about showing up at practice, then he was answering the intercom. And the next thing they knew, the boy was handing them two enormous burlap bags, and Ned was waving goodbye.

"Well, what was I supposed to say?" Nick asked, trying to heave his bag onto his bike basket, "I need half a cup of sawdust today to fool the real estate inspector?"

Lucy pulled hard on the pedals of her bike. "Nick, this stuff weighs a ton!"

"Well, what'd you expect? You can't just put down a fistful for chickens!" Then he started laughing.

Lucy laughed too even though she didn't want to. It made her bike wobble even more.

They laughed all the way to Molly Pitcher Park, where they dumped most of the sawdust in the flower beds, for mulch.

♋   ♋   ♋

At home Mom was in the kitchen doing her annual batch of cherry jam.

"Finally! Some luck!" whispered Nick. Lucy knew what he meant. When Mom made jam, she stayed close to the stove and sort of disappeared behind a cloud of steam for an hour or two. Still, Lucy hesitated by the kitchen door. She was hungry—and those big bowls of cherries were making her mouth water.

"Later Lu. If we go in now, she'll hand us knives, and we'll end up having to chop. C'mon. All we need to do is sprinkle a little sawdust, spray a few leak marks and glue a window or two. That shouldn't take long."

But Nick was wrong. They kept running into complications. Like the squirt gun. Who would have thought Winnie took it to wet her curls down? It took half an hour to figure that out. Then they had to line up the plumbing to decide where the leaks should be. Then when they sprayed the squirt gun, you could tell the marks were new because of the way they dripped into the old dust. So they had to find rags—make them, rather, since all the clean ones were in the kitchen with Mom—and clean the walls off. Also, the floor leaks turned out faky-looking. A brown magic marker dipped around the edges aged them nicely, but discovering that trick took time too.

Then there were the fights. The first one was over the sawdust. They could both see it looked awfully fresh. They agreed they'd have to mix it with stuff on the ground where last winter's wood pile was. But Nick found a couple of bugs there that looked like real termites and wanted to bring them inside. Lucy said was he crazy. Nick asked if she really cared about Sapphire. Thinking about Sapphire made Lucy's eyes fill up. Nick hurriedly offered to kill the bugs first, and Lucy asked "How could you?" In the meantime, the bugs escaped. So that fight was over.

The window one went on much longer. Nick wanted to glue lots of windows. "The more the better," he'd said. "Mr. Wickfield will think the house is hopeless." Lucy said maybe they'd better do just a few because what if they couldn't get them unglued. Then they fought about which ones. Nick wanted to do Lucy's, and Lucy said, "do your own." In the end they compromised, doing both of theirs a little and the hall and the stair one more heavily.

When they were finally finished, it was past noon, and they were tired and hungry. Downstairs the kitchen window was wide open, a breeze was blowing in, and a dozen shiny jars of crimson-colored jam were sitting on the counter. Mother was nowhere in sight. The bowls of cherries were nowhere in sight either. Lucy couldn't even find leftovers. She sighed, joining Nick over at the bread box, waiting for him to hand her the knife.

While she fixed a tuna fish sandwich, she thought about the Dourmans. What if they didn't care if there were termites? What if they'd figured on an exterminator anyway? They could certainly afford one.

She was about to say this to Nick, and stopped. He looked so ridiculous. His cheeks were stuffed, but you could still tell he was smiling. Every few minutes he'd shake his head, dreaming of Mr. Wickfield's reactions, no doubt. She took a bite of her sandwich.

Nick washed the last of his down with a gulp of milk, then announced: "Lucy, we did a great job on the downstairs bathroom, don't you think? I mean, it looks so gross..."

Lucy smiled in spite of herself, but just then, through the open window, came that familiar squawk. She stood up. Through the open window, she could just make out the light spot on the creek that was Sapphire. She was still swimming in circles.

Lucy wanted more than anything then to go down and comfort her duck, but suddenly there was a knock at the back door. Then Mr. Wickfield was there, Mother was there, and Nick was standing up, shaking hands.

"And this is my daughter Lucy," Mom was saying. Lucy looked at her Mom. She was all dressed up, earrings even. Where was she going?

"I'm happy to meet you," Mr. Wickfield said, grinning like the Cheshire cat, and looking both too tall and too overdressed for crawling through attics or hunching under plumbing fixtures. He wore a grey suit which hung loosely on his bony frame and carried a black folder.

Lucy smiled back, then squirmed as he continued to stare at her. Was he trying to think of something else to say? Would it be impolite to take another bite of her sandwich while he was looking at her? But then he cleared his throat and turned back to Mom. "This won't take long. I'll just be checking over the general condition of the structure and making estimates of any necessary repairs for the Dourmans." He hesitated, then quickly added, as if he didn't care, "Will I be bothering you around the house this afternoon?"

"No, Mr. Wickfield," Mom said, glancing at her watch. "I've got a portrait sitting at 1:00, my eldest is at a dance workshop, and the two little ones will be on an errand for me."

Lucy nearly choked on her tuna. Errand? What errand? Nick threw her a wide-eyed, questioning look. Mr. Wickfield beamed.

"Lucy and Nick may be back before you're gone. If you have questions, and they can't answer them, feel free to call me." She handed Nick her watercolor boards and Lucy her palette to take to the car. "Stay there a minute," she whispered, then she took out a piece of paper and began to write down a phone number.

While they waited, they could hear Mr. Wickfield turn the kitchen faucet on and off, flush the downstairs toilet. Then Mom was there, pulling a slip of paper from her purse.

"Would you kids get this stuff from Bixler's? Ingredients for brownies," she explained. "And make a large batch when you get back, OK? The art group's meeting at our house tonight." She paused, then added quietly, "If you hurry, you should be back in half an hour. Quite frankly, I'd feel better if someone was here when Mr. Wickfield leaves. Make sure he doesn't walk away with the TV or something, OK? Oh, I'll be at Mrs. Phillip's house, if you need me. I'm painting her cat."

Nick hooted, slapping his knee. "Really?"

Lucy failed to see the humor. I think Mrs. Phillip's white cat would make a great painting. He's gorgeous."

"Well, I hope he's as well-behaved as he is gorgeous. And speaking of well-behaved, don't pester Mr. Wickfield and don't get in his way. Understand?"

"Right," Nick answered.

"Right," echoed Lucy.

They both waved until Mom pulled out of the driveway, then they flipped one of Nick's quarters, to see who'd watch and who'd go to the store.

In another five minutes Lucy was on her new bike, a streak of gold on the highway. They'd pretended to leave together, of course, in case Mr. Wickfield was watching. But then Nick parked his bike just east of their property line, in a thick clump of willows, and snuck back along the hill. "I wonder what he's doing now," Lucy thought, pedaling so hard her legs felt almost numb.

She imagined she'd broken a speed record by the time she got there, screeching to a halt just two inches short of the front door, alarming Mrs. Burkett who was just leaving with a bag of sweet corn.

Once inside, things went maddeningly slowly. Oren McCaleb was there and wanted to know if she had really seen a redhead at her place. What color bill did he have? What color eyes? What did he sound like? She tried to listen and answer politely, backing up half an aisle for the baking chocolate, smiling, reaching into the refrigerator's glass doors for milk, stooping to the lowest shelf for nuts. But sugar was on the last aisle. Could she still talk from two aisles over?

Luckily Jed Owen walked in, fishing pole in hand.

"Loafin' again, hey Jed?" said Mr. McCaleb.

"I've got to get sugar," Lucy said softly, not even looking to see if she'd been heard, taking off like a shot.

Seven minutes later she pulled off the road, parked her bike next to Nick's and reached into his basket for the white slip of paper that hadn't been there before.

"MEET ME BY THE COMPOST HEAP," it said. "AND BE CAREFUL. HE'S OUTSIDE!"

Lucy stopped hesitantly at the top of the driveway, crouching slightly behind a thick clump of weeds. She couldn't see Mr. Wickfield, but she heard a dull thump-thumping sound coming from the shed, then "Psst. Lucy! Lu!"

It was Nick, running toward her, low, from the compost pile through the wild raspberry bushes, his cheeks flushed, his white T-shirt stained with berry juice and dirt.

"He's in the shed," he whispered to her from the bottom of the other side of the driveway. Then, looking back to make sure it was safe, he ran up and across to her, grabbing her arm, pulling her back in the direction of the bikes.

"Lucy!" He stopped to catch his breath, then began again. "Lucy, you aren't going to believe this in a million years!..."

CHAPTER NINE

DISCOVERIES

Nick began waving his hands, talking fast. "Lu, he's got a metal detector! He went all over the meadow with it, then the field, the groundhog holes, everywhere. He even checked over by the frog pond!"

"A metal detector? You mean like the thing Markie Anders got for Christmas that finds coins and buried treasure?"

"Exactly. But I don't think he found anything. He put it back and locked his trunk. And he hasn't done any digging. At least not yet. He's in the shed now. And he didn't start with all that thumping. First he looked through all those old boxes in the back part."

"Wow!" Lucy said quietly, trying to take it all in. "What's he looking for anyway?"

"I don't know," Nick replied, "but we better get back before he finds it."

The two children made sure to make lots of noise as they rode their bikes back down the drive.

"Let's get going on those brownies," Nick said in a loud voice.

"Right," Lucy answered, thumping her bike down on the ground, slamming the back door after her.

"Take your post in the cellar," Nick told her quietly as she set the groceries down. "I'll keep an eye on him outside."

Lucy hated the cellar. And she hated this corner behind the canning jars even more. The air smelled musky and damp. She had broken at least one spider web getting in and there were others all around her. She crouched uneasily, looking around for the homeless spider, seeing only a hundred legger crawling a couple of inches in front of her feet. Lucy shuddered, suddenly glad for her too-tight tennis shoes.

Mr. Wickfield bent his head as he entered the small, dirt-floored cellar. Lucy could see the light bulb cord in front of him, but he must have just come inside from the bright outdoors because he felt about for it as if he were blind.

Lucy crouched lower when the light went on, but she could still see him through two old coffee cans, looking at the furnace up close, taking a note, looking at the walls, touching them, making a note, looking at the floors, kicking at the sawdust, scooping up a bit, smelling it...

"Drats!" thought Lucy. They had gotten it to look old all right, but even she could smell the freshness of it, way over here. He took a hammer out from his back pocket now, knocked on the walls just above the pile at his feet, tugged at the timber in front of him, kicked it. The he made another mark in his folder.

He started knocking on the walls all over now—low, medium, up toward the ceiling. Like a man with a xylophone, Lucy thought, as he walked around, playing the walls, bending and unbending. Lucy held her breath as he came to the old shelves of canning jars. She could feel the air move above her head as the hammer thudded just above her. But he didn't stop. He didn't see her. She was safe. When she looked up he was pulling a metal tape measure from his pocket.

Mr. Wickfield measured the stairs, the walls, even the floor. He stopped after doing the boarded-door that led to the outside laundry room under the summer kitchen, and stood for a minute or two, stroking his chin thoughtfully, then turned and walked quickly back up the stairs.

Lucy peeked into the kitchen a minute later.

"He's outside again," Nick said, setting the electric mixer down too fast, spraying chocolate batter onto the wall.

"I think he's headed for the laundry room," Lucy said quietly. "The door seemed to interest him."

"Did he notice the sawdust?"

"He smelled it even, and I think he knew it was fresh, but he went thumping on all the walls anyway. Then he made a mark in his book, but I couldn't see what it was. He really is acting peculiar, Nick."

Lucy was just about to leave for the laundry room when she felt a hand on her back. She nearly jumped out of her skin. It was Mr. Wickfield, tapping her on the shoulder. Without his thumpy hammer, he moved as stealthily as a cat.

"You two just go on with your...uh...chore," he said, smiling nervously. "I'll just be in the dining room. I've got to check the...uh...fireplace."

Lucy helped Nick grease the pans and pour the batter, listening carefully to the usual thumping. When that stopped, they forgot all about clean-up, and peaked from behind the dining room door.

He was trying the windows. Good! That meant he'd be trying the ones upstairs too and would have to tell the Dourmans they wouldn't open.

The fireplace, though, seemed to be what most interested him, especially the old gun cupboard that sat right inside one wall of the chimney. He opened and closed it a dozen times, tapping, then pounding on its inside walls. When he finally finished that, he got down on his hands and knees and began tugging on the bricks inside the hearth. Then, without saying a word, he brushed off his hands, left the room, and headed up the stairs. In a minute they heard his footsteps in Mom and Dad's room.

"He's following the chimney up, I bet!" said Lucy. "You take Mom's room. I'll wait in the attic."

When they got to the landing, they could see him through the open bedroom door. He was on his hands and knees again with his tape measure. Nick said he'd wait there and run back down quickly when Mr. Wickfield was done. Lucy went on, opened the door to the attic stairs—but only slightly, remembering how it squeaked—crossed her fingers to signal good luck to Nick, then slipped in sideways. She began tiptoeing up, very quietly, skipping the third step because she knew it would creak, then taking the stairs two at a time, glad again for her tennis shoes which didn't make a sound on the old wood.

Hot air engulfed her at the top and she stopped for a second, feeling weak, wondering where she'd hide. She certainly couldn't take the trunk. He'd be sure to rummage through it. Then she remembered the drop cloths for painting. She'd seen Dad take them up right after he finished the living room last summer. There—there they were, folded up neatly behind the packing boxes, next to Nick's old trike. She ran over quickly, spreading them as messily as she could, and crawled underneath—just in time too. Mr. Wickfield was on the stairs.

He made straight for the far side of the attic and looked around carefully as he took his jacket off. He felt a few of the wooden beams with his hands, stared at the floor, kicked at the fake termite sawdust again, then headed toward the chimney, notebook in hand, marking as he walked.

When he got there he set his coat and notebook down, then frowned at the old bricks. The chimney up here seemed to be a disappointment to him, but he faithfully measured and poked at it anyway, then turned away and began sliding his tape measure along the walls.

Lucy realized she was right in his path and tried silently to scooch up unnoticed. When Mr. Wickfield got to her he stepped on parts of the canvas, but luckily not on Lucy. She breathed a sigh of relief.

By the time Mr. Wickfield went through the door to the adjoining, smaller attic, she knew exactly what he'd do next. She also knew what she would do. Measuring wouldn't take long. But soon he'd come back for his hammer. When he re-entered that other attic she'd have at least three minutes...

Lucy waited quietly, her heart beating so loudly she was afraid he could hear it. Sure enough, there he was, grabbing his mallet, knocking at the walls, nearing the door, gone.

Now! Lucy threw off her cover and ran tiptoe to Mr. Wickfield's notebook, which he'd left on the floor by the chimney. She crouched down low, her head just inches from the floor, so she could easily read the open pages. On the right hand side was a list with columns: "Electrical Systems," "Heating System," "Plumbing," "Insulation." Underneath were little boxes to check and questions that seemed just right for a real estate inspector, like "What kind of heating system?" "How old?" "Output." There were blank pages on the left under a huge heading that said "NOTES" and lying on top of these empty pages were two, loose, folded ones.

Lucy opened the top one. She realized almost immediately that she was looking at a map of their house, a sort of bird's eyes view, for there to the east was the creek, curving down almost to the highway. The house itself was a big square. The little circle next to it, she guessed, must be the old walnut tree. But what were these squares of broken lines?—one out in the frog pond, one big one in the meadow, one by the old groundhog's hole—just the places Nick said he'd been looking!

She opened the next paper quickly, for Mr. Wickfield's hammering was coming closer now. This one was a set of blueprints, three on the page—one for each story. Mr. Wickfield had been writing down all those measurements right here. The question marks looked fresh too, for they were in the same color ink—one by the dining room chimney, one by the boarded-up cellar door, and one by Mom's closet.

He was very close now; she could hear his footsteps. She folded the two papers back up and set them down at the same angle they'd been before. But wait. There wasn't any writing on them before. She picked the folded paper up, trembling. The scribbled note read: "Be sure to check possible sites for old springhouse." Puzzled, Lucy turned it to its white side, the way it was before, then got up and scurried silently across the floor toward the stairs.

She almost fell smack into Nick at the landing.

"Well?"

"Well, I saw his folder, and he put a check by leaks, and a question mark by termite damage. But listen, Nick! He's also got a map of the house in that folder! With little boxes in the meadow and the frog pond and the field—and question marks all over the house!"

Lucy spoke quickly as they headed downstairs, afraid she would forget some detail if she didn't tell it all at once. She ended up with the scratched note about the springhouse.

For a long time, they sat quietly by the dining room table, taking it all in. Lucy was drenched with sweat from being in the attic, and now the breeze from the window was cooling her off deliciously. After two brownies and a cold glass of milk, she didn't feel tired or shaky anymore.

"What do you suppose those broken boxes mean?" Lucy asked.

"Well, he's more than just a real estate inspector, that's for sure." After a minute Nick added, "That note about the springhouse just kills me. Imagine. He's checking on something that isn't even there anymore. What's he looking for, anyway?"

"I don't know," Lucy answered, "but I know who might."

CHAPTER TEN

DOING THE RIGHT THING

Friday morning was farmers' market, and they couldn't get out of that—Mom said she needed the extra hands. Which was true. Nick ended up with a chin-high bag of string beans and two cantaloupes. Lucy carried a huge bouquet of daisies, warm doughnuts from the Kreider bakery stall, and a sack of peaches. Mom had cukes, dill, new potatoes and tomatoes.

On the way home, she munched on a doughnut and tried to figure out how they were going to get over to Mrs. Rummel's instead of cleaning vegetables.

Mom interrupted her thoughts. "You two think you could wash this stuff and put it away without me? I have to meet Daddy at noon. We have a couple of appointments in Mount Holly to see apartments."

The word "apartments" made Lucy's stomach go tight, but at least her Mom would be gone. She asked if they could go bike riding when they were done.

They found Mrs. Rummel sitting in the middle of her kitchen, looking like a lady at a bake sale. She was surrounded by sugar cookies, gingerbread, funnel cakes and pretzels. Also next to her was a pink-wrapped present, brown paper and string, and a box of plastic bags.

Her eyes went wide with surprise when Elva showed them in. She eagerly waved them forward. "What luck! You're back so soon!"

"What are you doing with all this stuff?" Nick began unceremoniously, sitting down next to the paper and twine. "Boy those funnel cakes sure look good."

Lucy frowned at her brother, but Mrs. Rummel only laughed. "Lucy, dear, you'd have to be a saint to resist Elva's funnel cakes. And my gingerbread isn't so easy to turn down either. You'll see. But first I have to get a box ready. My granddaughter Rachel will be four next Thursday, so we've got to hurry this out—the doll, the cookies... How are you two at packing anyway?"

So they got to work. Waiting for the cookies was easy, but waiting for answers wasn't. Lucy was so excited her hands shook as she placed the cookies, back to back, inside the bags and wrapped them with crumpled tissue, talking quickly all the while, first about Sapphire's trip to the duck pond, because Mrs. Rummel had asked about her pet, but then about Mr. Wickfield and his strange behavior.

Nick was keyed up and acting silly. He began to creep around, hunched over, knocking on the walls, on the cupboards, on Mrs. Rummel's refrigerator. Every once and a while he'd stop, show his teeth in a ridiculous grin and mumble "I just wanted to check... the... uh... woodwork."

Mrs. Rummel laughed so hard she had to pull a hanky from her pocket to dab at her eyes. But she stopped when she glanced at Lucy. "Oh Lucy, I know exactly what your Mr. Wickfield is. He's a fortune hunter—and a very amateurish and sneaky one at that. Just one more fool looking for the Silverling Treasure."

The word "treasure" seemed to fill the air, ringing in their ears like silver.

Mrs. Rummel looked first at Lucy, who was still blinking in surprise, then at Nick, who was suddenly unhunched, his mouth wide open. She frowned, then looked at her lap, mumbling something about her big mouth.

"What kind of treasure?" Lucy asked breathlessly.

"Are you saying there's...like...a treasure hidden in our house?" Nick squeaked.

Mrs. Rummel was shaking her head now. "I think it's time for a break," she said, ignoring their questions, ordering Nick to the cellar for cider and Lucy to the pantry for "leftovers" from the morning's baking.

By the time they got back, she'd already pushed the packing things off to one side and put out clean plates. She asked Nick to pour the cider, while she filled them with one of everything, still ignoring the questions, which had started up again.

She picked up a pretzel. "I apologize for bringing it up—about the treasure, I mean. It's just the kind of story that could give two kids in need of money a whole lot of false hope. Trust me, children. There isn't any treasure to find."

"But you have to tell us about it!" Lucy said.

"You could at least tell us!" Nick echoed. "We're going to die of curiosity."

Mrs. Rummel laughed. "Well, we couldn't have that. And since I brought it up, I guess I'm going to have to tell you. Then you'll see. At least you'll understand about that foolish young man. Go on, now," she added, looking at them. "How can you resist these cookies?"

But they didn't start eating until she started talking again.

"Do you children remember when I told you about my grandmother, Lucy Silverling?"

"Sure," Nick answered. "She was skinny as a broom and lived in our house and had ducks."

Mrs. Rummel nodded. "I didn't tell you everything about her though. I didn't tell you about how she was orphaned."

"Orphaned?" Nick asked. "You mean her parents died?"

Mrs. Rummel nodded. "One Sunday afternoon when she was, oh, about your age, Lucy, her mom and dad went off for a carriage ride and never came back. It was a freak accident—a sudden storm—lightning. The horse must have bolted. They found them the following day at the bottom of a deep ravine."

Lucy shivered. And she'd been thinking they were having troubles.

"Anyway," Mrs. Rummel continued, "when that happened, the relatives came for Lucy and since there were no bank accounts and no will, they decided that Emmet and Katryn's money must be hidden somewhere in the house. They searched everywhere, for this would have been part of Lucy's inheritance. But it was never found. That was the money that came to be known as the 'Silverling Treasure.'"

"Wow!" said Nick, waving his pink-frosted gingerbread man, "who'd have thought anybody that lived in our old house would have money."

Mrs. Rummel looked amused. "It wasn't a lot of money. Emmet Silverling wasn't rich in that way. His wealth was in his land and in his large, comfortable house." She glanced at Nick, then with a twinkle in her eye, added, "not fancy, as you suggested, but certainly roomy and built to last. He must have had some cash though. He earned it on the side as a cabinet maker. That was his father's trade, and he learned it well. Some say he was better at it than his own dad. But this money could only have been a modest amount—savings for a rainy day. Something like what your own parents probably have in their savings account."

"And they're sure not rich," Lucy said with a sigh, swirling the tip of her cookie in her cider. "Not rich enough to buy a certain farmhouse."

"Wait a minute," Nick butted in. "If there's hardly any money, then how come Mr. Wickfield is so hot to find it? How come they call it a treasure?"

"That was the name of the article old Mr. Glenerry wrote: 'Hidden Treasures of South Middleton.' He named four families who seemed to have missing money. He guessed it would be in nineteenth century coins. Some of those really are a treasure—to collectors. They pay astonishing amounts of money for rare ones, you know."

"Coins!" exclaimed Lucy.

"That's why he had the metal detector!" Nick jumped up from his chair. "Lucy we've got to get going."

Mrs. Rummel's cheeks went red. She lifted her hand. "Just sit right down young man, and listen to what I'm trying to tell you. Four generations of my family have searched for that money. I spent half my own childhood looking. Don't you think that if there were any money, we would have found it by now?"

"Maybe not," said Nick. I mean, they didn't have metal detectors and stuff in those days, did they?

Mrs. Rummel sighed. "It's more complicated than that. There are other things to consider."

They waited.

"Lucy's parents died during the Civil War. The Confederate army was marching north. People then were terribly concerned about their homes and their property.

Some people say Lucy's parents' ride into the woods was to hide the very treasure you're thinking of looking for. So it might never have been hidden at the house."

Lucy and Nick looked at each other but didn't say anything.

"Besides, there's always the possibility that a family member found it during the great search and simply pocketed it for himself."

Lucy and Nick nodded, but they still didn't say anything.

"Even if it's there, the coins may not be valuable. Not every old coin is, you know. Anyway," she concluded, "you'd have to find it first, and that, like I said before, is just not possible."

Nick stared into his cider. Then he started smiling. Lucy had this picture in her mind: telling Sapphire Mrs. Rummel had a treasure now, that they wouldn't need to move after all, and she broke into a smile too. "I can't help it," she told Mrs. Rummel. "I can't help hoping."

"Tell us where you looked, Mrs. Rummel. Then we won't waste any time there."

Lucy leaned closer, to hear better.

"It's these cookies," Nick said, seeing her stern face. "They make you feel like...like...Superman."

"Sherlock Holmes," added Lucy.

"The Pink Panther," added Mrs. Rummel, rolling her eyes. All three of them burst out laughing, but the old lady ended by shaking her head sadly.

"I should never have told you," she began. "But now I see you're going to have to get this out of your system. And it's going to disappoint you. And it's all my fault." She sighed again, then sat up a little straighter. "I will tell you where I looked, but first I want you to promise me, Lucy, you will get Sapphire back to the pond and try again."

"Dad already made me promise," said Lucy. "I know I have to."

"Well... all right then," Mrs. Rummel said. Let's see. It's only been more than fifty years." She closed her eyes and raised a finger to her lips, tapping softly. Her eyes looked a little watery when she finally opened them. "I did enjoy those days with Gram. I had a swing under the walnut tree..."

"We do too!" Lucy and Nick said together.

Mrs. Rummel leaned back into her chair. She was smiling a little now, as if looking back at happy times. "I know I did everything your Mr. Wickfield did. I measured the outside and the inside walls and pounded them trying to find hollow spaces. I checked for loose bricks in the fireplace and all up and down the chimney. And for loose boards in the floor. I used to dig a lot too, especially on muddy days when it was easier. Gram would get so mad.

I used to dig by the old barn and springhouse. When I was small there were still parts of the foundation showing."

"I didn't know there used to be a barn," Nick said. "And what exactly is a springhouse, anyway?"

The barn was where the meadow garden is now and burned down before I was born. The springhouse was off to the south of it. You'd know where it was just by looking for running water in the reeds. Springhouses were places built over flowing water where farmers could keep their milk and other perishable foods cool and fresh."

"The frog pond!" exclaimed Lucy. She turned to Mrs. Rummel and explained, "That's what we call it, even though it isn't a pond at all—just a damp boggy place where lots of frogs live. Mr. Wickfield was digging there too! Do you think it could be there?"

"I think any outbuilding would be a good hiding place and that Mr. Wickfield knows it. He also knows it could be in a hundred other places as well, and from what you've said, he's checked a lot of them already."

Lucy sighed. Nick drummed his fingers on the table. This was going to be a big job.

Mrs. Rummel put a hand on Lucy's hair. If Grandma would want anyone to have her own treasure, I'm sure it would be someone like you. Then she winked at Lucy and actually said something encouraging: "Maybe she'll leave you a clue."

♋   ♋   ♋

Lucy's mind was buzzing as they finally taped the packing box shut. She could hardly wait to get home and start searching. She knew it seemed hopeless to Mrs. Rummel. But it was a chance, at saving their house. Sapphire. They had to try.

Mrs. Rummel was obviously thinking her own thoughts as she picked up a marker and wrote the address. When she'd finished printing the word WYOMING, she put the pen down and sighed. "I do wish they wouldn't have moved so far away. I wish my John's wife Becky would have liked it better here in the East."

She shook her head as if shaking sad thoughts away and smiled at Lucy and Nick. "But then I never would have met you. And you are special friends."

Nick looked puzzled. "How come their moving away made you know us?"

"Oh. I guess I didn't tell you. John and Becky lived in your house while he finished his degree at Dickinson College. They had little Rachel right here in Pennsylvania. But Becky's from the West and missed it terribly, and John had a job offer in Sheridan—with a coal company. So they left. And suddenly the house we'd worked so hard to fix up for them was empty again. Suddenly it seemed right to have another family there. That's when we rented it to you."

"Is that their stuff in the attic then?" Lucy asked.

"What stuff?" Mrs. Rummel asked. "I thought they'd taken everything with them. Otto said he'd checked the place over before you moved in."

"There's not anything," Nick answered. Just some old papers and a mailbox."

"There's a lovely big bed, though," Lucy added. "It's wonderful!"

Mrs. Rummel looked surprised. Then her forehead crinkled and her lips turned downward in a frown.

"What's wrong?" Lucy asked.

"It's nothing. I guess Otto didn't want to disappoint me—to tell me right away. And then he had the stroke and couldn't tell me."

"Tell you what?"

"That they didn't want the bed. We gave it to them— for Rachel. Becky and John bought all modern furniture when they first married. Still, we thought Rachel might like to use her great-great-grandmother Lucy's bed. We told the kids if they didn't think they could use it they should just leave it there, and Otto would bring it back. I guess those two young ones just aren't sentimental, like me," said Mrs. Rummel, looking at her lap.

Secretly Lucy thought—"How could they be so ungrateful?" But out loud she only said, "If I had a bed like that I'd feel like Queen of the May!" She told Mrs. Rummel about her own secondhand bed, about how its white coat of paint was peeling, and how she'd patched it with funny stickers.

"I know what you mean about feeling like a queen," Mrs. Rummel said, getting a faraway look in her eye. "When I stayed with Gram, I used to sleep in that bed and it's just how I felt. Like a princess in a fairy tale. You know, her own dad made it for her. He carved the flowers and birds on it, one by one, just for Lucy. When I was little I used to think it was magic, that all those designs would come alive one night, that the birds would line up on the window sill and sing good morning and the flowers would be fresh on the pillow when I opened my eyes. Isn't that silly?"

"Yes," said Nick, just as Lucy said, "No." All three of them laughed.

Mrs. Rummel looked at Lucy then in a way that reminded Lucy of her own grandmother. Suddenly she felt she knew exactly what Mrs. Rummel was thinking. The words simply fell from her lips.

"You'd like to see it again, wouldn't you? Before it's the Dourmans' and all changed. Before it's gone forever."

Lucy knew then she had to decide something—and quickly. She took a deep breath and blurted it out. "We want you to come."

Nick looked at her in disbelief. His eyes were big as saucers.

"I'd like to. Yes. But it's really hard for me to get around..."

"We understand," Nick said.

"We'll pick you up," Lucy suggested. "And Nick and I will make our special brownies, won't we, Nick?"

"Uh... sure. Sure," Nick answered, smiling weakly at Mrs. Rummel. But when she turned back to Lucy his eyes were on the ceiling. He looked exasperated.

"I'll have Mom call you," Lucy added.

Mrs. Rummel beamed. Nick looked at her like she'd lost her mind.

"Oh, come on, Nick," Lucy whispered as they walked outside. "We were going to have to tell Mom sooner or later anyway. Don't you remember we offered to help her last time—with errands and stuff."

"Yeah, well you might at least have waited until after the Dillsburg game. If we get grounded and I don't show up, the guys will probably never speak to me again."

"We did the right thing," Lucy said stubbornly.

"Who says we didn't?" Nick snapped back, hopping on his bike. "Let's just get it straight who gets the credit for it." And with that he pulled away, never looking back.

Lucy sighed as she got on her own bike. Mom couldn't be angry with her for doing the right thing. Could she?

CHAPTER ELEVEN

THE HUNT

Lucy was so worried about what Mom would say that she went straight to find her, before she lost her nerve. On her path toward the creek Misty seemed to materialize smack in front of her. She almost tripped over him. She took a couple of drunken, running steps before she caught her balance, then looked back in annoyance. She blinked.

Sometimes that duck looked so... so hazy—as if he were painted on the surface of her thoughts and wasn't there at all. She squinted, wondering if she might need glasses, but then she realized that was ridiculous. She could see him perfectly, down to the stripes on those grey feathers, the ring of gold in his eye.

"We'll find the treasure, Lucy. Don't worry. Believe me. Do you believe?"

Her heart did a little flip and she took a few steps back toward him, listening for more. But there wasn't more. There was never any more. She stared at him, full of wonder at how those thoughts came, just from looking at him, then seemed to stop in mid-air, as if he were waiting for something. But what?

She stared at that skinny, red head, and chills prickled up her neck. Lit by the overhead sun, he looked as beautiful and other-worldly as he had on the first night. But then she remembered what Dad said—about hundreds of other ducks, who looked just like him.

The sun slipped under a cloud for a minute, just a minute, and in that dark and ordinary light she realized something: Misty seemed to repeat things she was already thinking or worrying about. Help with her problem. Money for a house. And now, treasure. The very thing she'd been thinking of all morning.

Was that what Misty was—some kind of mental mirror? The sun came back out, making those gold eyes shine at her again. But the magic was gone now. She turned back onto the path, thinking of things she was sure of—like the Silverling money, and what they could do about it. And then about another sure thing—the way Mom was bound to react to her news. She took a deep breath and almost ran down the hill anyway.

Mom was doing maybe her hundredth painting of the Yellow Breeches. She was concentrating hard, but not so hard she couldn't hear Lucy behind her. "What's up, pumpkin?" she asked, setting down her brush and turning around.

The speech inside Lucy's head broke like a bubble. She couldn't remember a word. So she just plunged in:

"I've been to see Mrs. Rummel. Twice. Nick came too, but it was my idea. We went when we should have been swimming. And this afternoon. It didn't do any good—about the house, I mean. But she's our friend now. She's nice. She...I...I invited her for a visit. I said you'd call her."

For a moment Mom looked too surprised to speak. Then she got that curious expression—like the one she'd had the first time Lucy wanted to jump off the high dive. Then a wave of anger clouded her features. Then the questions started. The comments: "That was lying!" "That was interfering!" and "Lucy Peterson, what if something had happened to you two. We'd never even know where to look. To begin to look!" She looked so disgusted that Lucy's eyes filled up.

81

She added softly, "I know how you feel about moving, Lucy. But before going off like that you should have checked with me...or Dad."

"But you would have said no!" Lucy yelled. "I had to go. I had to. I had to do something to help Sapphire. Oh, Mom," she added, the tears really coming now, "I can't just leave her here. All by herself. Don't you see?"

Lucy turned, shamed by the tears, wiping them away, though they just kept welling up and spilling over. Suddenly it was as if moving day were today. It was that real. She headed for the shallows, where she'd just heard Sapphire. She sat down on the shore and waited, wiping her eyes with the bottom of her T-shirt. Then she was holding her duck, bending over her, wishing she never had to get up. That she could stay here forever.

Mom came over and sat down. She started plucking up blades of grass, not saying anything.

Lucy finally turned to her. "I know this sounds crazy, Mom—because of everything you tell us about interfering and all. But deep down I thought maybe you wanted Mrs. Rummel to know."

Her mom just looked at her. "Lucy, Lucy," she said softly. "My little mind reader." Then she looked out at the water. In that little gold-lit corner it seemed impossible there could be a sad thought. But now it looked like even Mom was about to cry. "I love this place, too, you know."

"There might be a chance, Mom," Lucy whispered.

Lucy's mom sighed. "Lucy, don't do this to yourself."

"Mom, for once in your life, you've got to listen to me like maybe I could know something, like maybe I'm half-way grown up and not just a dumb kid."

Lucy's Mom looked surprised, but she said "OK. I'm listening. Say whatever you want. I'll hear you out. I give my word."

"Mom, Nick and I found out there might be a treasure hidden in our house..."

Mom winced. Her eyes filled up.

"Mom I mean it..."

"Did I say anything? Go ahead."

So Lucy told everything. And Mom listened, though she looked a little skeptical hearing about Bluebill's resemblance to Misty. She laughed though, at the Mr. Wickfield parts of the story, and her eyes got big as buttons when Lucy told her that Mrs. Rummel said the treasure was real.

"So you see, there is a chance," Lucy finished. "You believe me don't you?" she added, into the silence. Mom, I told you, this is real."

"Well," her mom repeated slowly. "Of course I believe you. And it is a chance. But only a one in a million chance. You know that don't you?" She got up, brushing the grass off her jeans. "Oh boy. Wait till your dad hears this."

The creek was red with sunset, and the shadows were long on the grass when the two of them finally opened the back door.

Dad was by the stove. "I started cooking without you—nothing fancy, you understand, just the creamiest, heartiest, most delicious potato soup in the universe." He licked the end of his wooden spoon, closing his eyes to savor the taste. "Magnifico!"

"Right now oatmeal mush would taste magnifico to me," Mom said. "I'm starved."

"Me too!" said Lucy, heading for the dining room.

At supper Lucy told the story again, for Dad and Winnie. Nick interrupted a lot, whenever she forgot something important. Winnie kept slapping her spoon down, saying, "This is unreal."

Dad said basically the same thing. Only he meant it. "You kids have got to realize you're asking the impossible. You're just setting yourself up for a terrible disappointment."

"We're disappointed already," Winnie said. Everyone looked at her. There were tears in her eyes. "Well, I don't want to leave either."

"Maybe our children need to feel we'll hear them out and help them with this—100 per cent," said Mom quietly. "And then, when...if...we don't find it, they'll know their parents were behind them, that we tried, and then we can go on with no regrets."

Mom stared at Dad. Dad at Mom. Then Dad wondered out loud if A-OK rentals had metal detectors. The children broke into cheers.

∽   ∽   ∽

Nick cleared, Winnie washed, and Lucy wiped. Upstairs Mom was on the phone with Mrs. Rummel. Nobody spoke, hoping to catch a fragment of conversation, but all they could hear was occasional laughter. Finally Mom came down. She was smiling.

"She is nice, Lucy. You know, I don't think she was just being polite when she said how much she enjoyed you. She seems truly fond of you and Nick."

"Well?" said Lucy. "Is she coming?"

"Yes. For dinner. Monday evening."

Monday. That gave them tomorrow and the next day and part of the next. Wouldn't it be fun to say "Guess what we found?" when Mrs. Rummel came to the door?

Lucy lay awake that night, counting man-hours for searching. There weren't as many as she first thought, if she allowed for Dad's test correcting and Mom's deadline on her cat painting. And of course Lucy herself was in charge of Monday's meal, since the whole thing had been her idea. Mom had said to do something easy—something she'd done before. But Winnie suggested a dozen fancier menus. She'd said Lucy and Nick's brownies were too ordinary. "This is a gala event! Here!" she'd said, pointing to a picture in Mom's cookbook. "Peaches Flambe is what you ought to do."

Lucy and Nick had laughed till the tears came. It was on fire! Even after Winnie had glared at them and said sarcastically, "You wait till the fire's out before you eat it, dummies!" they would still giggle when they looked at each other. Now Lucy wasn't laughing. Maybe they ought to make something fancier than brownies.

That night she dreamed she made brownies, but when she set them on the table they burst into flame, the dining room filled with smoke, and the fire detectors in the kitchen and the upstairs hall started buzzing.

When she opened her eyes, they were still buzzing. Wait a minute. She threw on her robe and ran downstairs. The buzzing was coming from a vacuum-cleaner shaped machine that Dad was sweeping over three quarters on the linoleum floor.

"Dad! A metal detector!" she cried, throwing her arms around him. "You are the best dad in the universe. Wherever did you get it?"

Dad laughed and hugged her back with his free arm. "A-OK. And it's all ours till Monday morning."

"Is that all you have to do? Just push it around? Where should we look first? Can I try?"

Dad gave her the handle. "When you hear it get loud, look at the meter up here. It even tells how far away the metal is."

Lucy swept it over the floor, delighted.

"Before you ride away with our little gadget, Lucy, it might be a good idea to read the instruction booklet—and have a look at the library books I brought home. They're on the dining-room table."

Winnie took that as an order and grabbed the metal shaft out of Lucy's hand. "I'm going to try the living room, squirt. I've already done my homework."

Nick looked up as Lucy approached the table. He had an English muffin in one hand and *Successful Coin Hunting* in the other. "Hey Lucy, it says here this guy found 138 coins inside an old door. It was hollow!"

Looking at the bacon and muffins and jam made Lucy feel a little hollow herself. While she ate she looked through a book that had brownish photographs and told about secret stairways and safes behind hidden panels. Lucy didn't think their farmhouse was big enough for a secret staircase or fancy enough for a safe. She turned a few pages and saw more pictures: of chimneys and smokehouses and springhouses. All of them had been used as hiding places. And look, here it said money was hidden under window ledges too. Lucy made a mental note to check the windows.

After eating, Lucy signed up on the user chart Dad had made. They each took their own rooms, of course. Dad and Mom took the cellar and attic. Winnie was down for the outside, with Nick. Lucy wrote her name under Halls and under Summer Kitchen.

That day flew by, and so did the next. Since they had to share the machine, everyone just marked the places it buzzed with masking tape, then did their digging and prying later. They also used all the old-fashioned search methods, as Mr. Wickfield had. Anyone walking by the old house that weekend would have found it extremely noisy with all the pounding and knocking and pushing furniture around. Even after 10:00 on Saturday when the detector was officially not in use, one could still hear the machine in the attic, scraping over the splintery floorboards, while down in the cellar there was a rattling from moving crates of canning jars and thumping that sounded a lot like Mr. Wickfield's.

By late Sunday they'd found two buffalo nickels, ten very old pennies, Mom's sapphire earring that had been missing since March, two dozen rusty nails, the squirrels' winter cache of black walnuts, two rake heads, and the huge, rusted blade of an ancient plow.

By Monday noon, Lucy was beginning to give up hope. Her own time for searching had dwindled to almost nothing. She had had to go to Bixler's for ingredients in the morning, and now she had to think about dinner and fixing up the house. The rest of the family seemed to have used up their time too. Dad was back at work, Mom was out looking at apartments in Mount Holly, Winnie had to babysit Gordy Kuger again and Nick was scheduled to play baseball. Even the detector was gone.

Lucy stooped down and opened the cupboard where Mom kept the crockpot. She was feeling just as black and gloomy as that farthest corner.

"The Dourmans probably won't want it after they see Mr. Wickfield's report."

Lucy looked up, startled. Nick was in the doorway, dressed in his baseball uniform. He was tossing an apple in the air.

"If I could just believe that," Lucy answered, then it would be a whole lot easier to stay in this kitchen right now. I wanted to make tonight special for Mrs. Rummel, Nick, and...and it's hard to excited about cooking a dumb old dinner when I think how late it is—and how we haven't found anything...Sapphire."

"Then don't think about it," Nick snapped back. "Think about Mrs. Rummel."

Lucy glared. She felt like swatting him, even if he was right.

"C'mon, Luce. You know I care about Sapphire too. But worrying about it isn't going to help anything."

Now he sounded like Mom. Now she really felt like swatting him.

He eyed the wall clock, then Lucy. "Look," he finally said, swooping past her. "I'll make the brownies."

He started pulling out ingredients: baking chocolate, nuts, baking powder. "If we hurry we can have all the food done in no time. I have to leave pretty soon," he added, not even pausing to look at Lucy while he unwrapped the margarine and chocolate, "but you can straighten the house up fast. Then you can check out the shed or laundry room one more time."

Lucy watched as her brother pulled out the pan for melting, assembled the mixer, pulled out the mixing bowls. He was moving as fast as Charlie Chaplin in an old silent film. If it wasn't for the deathly serious look on his face, he'd look just as comical. She wondered what time his game started, but didn't dare ask.

Lucy turned back for the tomatoes and got out the can opener. They worked quietly then, only speaking to ask for the salt, or the margarine. It occurred to Lucy that she had the best brother in the world.

By the time Mom got back, the spaghetti sauce was cooking, dessert was done, and the house was clean. Lucy had put the white linen tablecloth on, set the table for six, and put out wine glasses for the grownups. In the center of the table she set two white candles in crystal holders and a bouquet of ivory roses from Mom's last year's Mother's Day bushes. Mom said the table looked elegant, dinner smelled wonderful and she'd be happy to finish up.

"Let's see. Pasta, garlic bread, salad, right? Oh, and Lucy, you better wash up and put something clean on. And just in case you're thinking of another round of treasure hunting, please avoid mudholes. And no digging!"

After washing, Lucy put on her blue running shorts, a white tank top, and her new thongs. Then she ran outside. In spite of Nick's help and her own rushing, it was already late. She wanted to search, but she just couldn't stay away from Sapphire one more minute.

The stream sounded curiously loud, like a morning after rain, but she could still make out Sapphire's quacking. When she reached the walnut tree, she stopped for a second, thinking of Mrs. Rummel and her old swing, but then she spotted Sapphire, waddling up from the water near the shallows. She ran down to her, holding out her arms. Sapphire stopped to quack her hello, then waddled straight into them.

"Oh, Sapphire, I missed you so much," she said, hugging her duck, stroking the top of her skinny head. Sitting in the sun with Sapphire, Lucy felt a rush of happiness. "I don't need to run around searching for treasure now," she said. "I'd much rather be with you Saph.

Anyway, there's no reason why we can't think about it and do the searching inside our heads, right now."

Sapphire looked at her, gave a little squawk and nipped her finger.

"So where do you suppose it is, Saph? We checked all the walls in the attic and all the floors, and all around the chimney. The detector didn't even peep. Pure nothing! And we didn't miss an inch either. Dad moved all the old boxes—even that heavy old bed—just so we could go over every single part of the wall. Nothing's up in the roof. It's only boards. You can see right through to the sky in places. No wonder it's so cold upstairs in the winter," she added, mostly to herself.

Sapphire slipped her beak beneath Lucy's folded hands, looking for food, obviously bored with the subject of treasures, but Lucy went on. "We did the cellar just as thoroughly. Of course, the furnace is new. For all we know, it might be buried under there, but we can hardly move it to find out. If it's there, it's just as good as there being no treasure at all."

The thought of that made Lucy feel panicky again. No treasure. No Sapphire. She hugged her pet tighter.

Just then she heard the car. It was Dad for sure. You could tell by the way the engine sputtered when he turned the key off. She put Sapphire down and ran part way up the hill to see if everyone was really there. Dad was supposed to pick Nick up at the park and get Winnie from the Kugers' before going on to Mrs. Rummel's. Well, there were enough people in the car, that's for sure. "Uh-oh," thought Lucy, as she counted heads. "I should have set for seven. Mrs. Schrader's here too!"

Dad helped Mrs. Rummel make her slow exit out the back door that faced Lucy. Nick held her walker. But

Mrs. Schrader popped right out the other side like bread from a toaster. She made a half circle around the car, peered up at the house, then down the hill. Shading her eyes from the afternoon sun, she craned her neck toward Lucy, then started marching briskly down the hill. She was pointing. "That duck," she said. "That duck. It's remarkable, Lucy."

CHAPTER TWELVE

NEWS AT DINNER

Lucy turned around, wondering what was so remarkable about Sapphire. She started at seeing Misty too, standing just yards away from her own duck! He was staring up at her matter-of-factly, as if he'd been there all afternoon.

Mrs. Schrader swept right by her, without so much as a nod, then knelt down, her back still ramrod-straight, in front of the red-headed duck. She stared at Misty. Misty stared back at her. A minute passed. Two. The old lady finally sat back on her heels and turned toward Lucy, staring again, the way she had at Misty. Lucy noticed her eyes for the first time. They were a startling, bright green.

"Is this why you were asking about Granny's Bluebill?" she asked brusquely.

"Yes, ma'm," Lucy answered nervously. She asked timidly, "Do you think they look alike?"

"Yes," Mrs. Schrader snapped back. "I do." Then she fired a half dozen questions at Lucy: "When did you first see him? Does he act peculiar? Did you notice he's wearing fall plumage in the middle of summer? Is he friendly?"

Lucy answered as quickly as she could, but she paused, quite astonished, when Mrs. Schrader asked her last question.

"Do you feel when he looks at you, Lucy, he's saying something?"

"Why... yes," Lucy finally answered, wide-eyed. "He said he'd come to help, that he knew we needed money, that we would find the..." She stopped, feeling her cheeks grow hot, realizing how ridiculous this must sound to a grownup.

But Mrs. Schrader didn't laugh. She didn't frown. What she did do was snap her fingers and finish for Lucy: "The treasure! I knew it!" She moved a little closer to Lucy and began speaking in a scratchy whisper, one long, bony finger waving in the air, as if her words were a song and she were conducting her own music.

"Lucy, I didn't remember until I saw the duck just now. And you know, I feel it was him—reminding me."

"Reminding you of what?" Lucy asked.

"Reminding me that Bluebill came back once."

"Came back?" Lucy squeaked. "You mean... after he..."

"Yes," Mrs. Schrader answered. "Grandma said it happened on her wedding day. In Boston, mind you. She was twenty-six. Bluebill should have been a very dead duck by then—or at least a very old and faraway one. But there he was, flying about the steeple—three times—just like he used to at home when there was a birthday or party or Lucy and he were just feeling happy."

Lucy followed Mrs. Schrader's waving finger up toward the house now, half expecting to see a white steeple instead of beech branches reaching toward the roof.

"Has he done that—around the chimney, I mean?" asked Mrs. Schrader, leaning even closer.

"No."

"Watch him," she replied. She shot up then, like a jack-in-the-box, turned, and began a rapid march back up the hill.

Lucy thought the conversation was over, but then she heard that brusk voice again, ringing out in short, snappy sentences. She ran to catch up.

"I've always been the sensible one, you know. I look at the evidence. Then I decide. Always believed in magic...ghosts. I know there are ghosts. Never mind what everyone else says. If you think straight, it's obvious."

Lucy's knees felt like they'd turned to jelly, but she managed to keep up, taking long, trembly steps. Nick was going to flip when he heard about Bluebill coming back.

The family was looking away from them. "And that was Elva's land," they heard Mrs. Rummel say as they came near the hilltop. Mrs. Rummel was standing in the middle of the back gate, looking very formal without her housecoat. Her dress was the color of wood violets. Lucy saw a shiny clasp and the muted sheen of pearls around her neck. Mom and Dad stood just behind her. Winnie and Nick were on either side, perched on the low fence inside spaces the wisteria had missed.

The group made no note of the two figures coming up the hill. They were listening intently to the old lady's voice, gazing in the direction of her trembling hand as it lifted momentarily from the silver walker toward the highway and the fields on the opposite side.

"Elva sold it before she moved to Scranton. That was years ago, before they widened the road. It's so noisy with the traffic now," she said sadly. But then she looked up and around and a smile lit her face. "The trees. The trees, though. My, they're even better than before."

"Hi, Mrs. Rummel," Lucy interrupted.

Suddenly the five faces that had been facing sky and leaves looked down at Lucy and Mrs. Schrader and then behind them. Lucy glanced back to see the ducks had followed. Sapphire was practically at her feet. Misty stood a few yards behind as still as a statue.

"My lovely Lucy!" exclaimed Mrs. Rummel. "Hello! And who are these? The lovely fatty is Sapphire, of course. My, look at those wings. What a beauty! But who's the other duck? Bluebill's ghost?"

Mrs. Schrader looked back at Lucy and raised an eyebrow. Lucy searched Mrs. Rummel's face. Did she believe too? But then the old lady burst into laughter. She was joking. "No wonder you asked about Bluebill. Where did you find this duck? I guess red-headed, blue-billed ducks are not from the land of magic, after all."

As they walked in, Mrs. Rummel explained about her grandma and how she liked to tell tall tales about her ducks. She said she thought her gran had surely made up the description of Bluebill. Mom and Dad laughed, and Dad added that redheads were actually quite common, even more so out west.

Lucy trailed behind, stopping at the back door. She stared at Misty through the screen. She heard Mom's voice drifting in from the dining room, "Lucy has a way with animals... She seems to know what they need...." Mrs. Rummel's faraway voice added, "Elva's that way too."

When Lucy got to the dining room everyone was oohing and aahing over the beautiful table and the wonderful smell of spaghetti sauce. Lucy blushed at the compliments, noticing thankfully that Mother had set an extra plate for Mrs. Schrader.

"We'd better taste it first, before we decide it's so good," she said, slipping in next to Nick, busying herself with her linen napkin, smoothing it on her lap.

As Mother began serving, everyone's attention turned to passing plates and breaking bread, and asking for the butter. Lucy relaxed and looked around. Mrs. Rummel was gazing around too, as if she were inside some wonderful dream. When their eyes met, Lucy smiled. She was glad she'd invited Mrs. Rummel.

Lucy stole a glance at Mrs. Schrader too. She was sitting straight-backed at the other side of the table, her electric white hair shooting out from under her hair combs. She seemed intent upon her noodles, winding them precisely around her fork, but she looked up, sensing Lucy's gaze. She smiled a smidgeon then, her lips barely turned upward No one would even know it was a smile, thought Lucy. Except me. We're going to be friends, she thought suddenly. And the thought seemed so crazy, she almost laughed out loud. Quickly she stuffed a piece of garlic bread in her mouth.

Supper conversation was lively. Nick was in a crazy mood because of the two home runs he'd hit. He told the story with so much arm waving that Lucy had to duck twice. Winnie reported on her afternoon too. She'd had to read *Paul Can Fly* four times before Gordy would take his nap.

Mrs. Rummel laughed. When she was little, she said, she drove her own mother crazy with the story of *Snow White and Rose Red.*

"You drove me crazy with it too," barked Mrs. Schrader. "I'm the one who always had to play it out with you afterward!"

"That's right," Mrs. Rummel said. "I was Rose and you were Snow White and Rover was the bear." They both laughed.

Lucy rested back in her chair after her second brownie. Mother had let her have a taste of wine, and now it burned warmly in the middle of her chest. She felt comfortable and a little drowsy. All the grownups seemed to be talking from far away now, about Mom's painting of the Yellow Breeches, then about Nick's talent as a dessert maker. Lucy was so relaxed and dreamy she almost missed what came next. Almost.

"My husband, John, would love these brownies, Nick. He's a real chocolate lover. If you give me the recipe, I can surprise him with a batch next week when I'm home again."

"You're going back to Scranton, then?" asked Dad.

"Yes, well, Hannah is mending nicely since her leg operation. And now the house is sold, she won't have any problem affording a practical nurse for the daytime...."

Lucy blinked her eyes. She sat up straight. Had Mrs. Schrader said "sold"? She looked at Mrs. Schrader, whose hand was over her mouth. She looked at Mrs. Rummel, who was glaring at her sister. She looked at Mom, whose cheeks were suddenly red, then at Dad, who was rubbing his forehead and shaking his head as if to say, "No.—Oh, no."

"Did you sell it, Mrs. Rummel?" Lucy asked, standing up. "Did you?"

"We were going to wait to tell you, Lucy," she said in a tired voice. She set her napkin down. "We didn't want to spoil this wonderful time you'd planned for everyone. I'm sorry, Lucy," she added in a whisper.

"The Dourmans?" Lucy asked feebly.

"I'm afraid so," Mrs. Rummel said. "They're coming Thursday to sign the papers."

"We're so sorry. Sorry... Sorry. "Mrs. Schrader, Mom, Dad. Everyone was saying it at once.

Lucy's knees felt like they were going to buckle, and she leaned on the table. She asked Mom when they'd have to leave.

"There's a lovely little brick townhouse that I just found today, Lucy. It's in Mount Holly on Plum Avenue. It'll be opening up in just three weeks—just in time for the new school year. It will be like a fresh beginning. I know you'll like it Lucy. There's a big common green with a giant oak. And the park's only two blocks away."

Lucy was backing up. "May I be excused?" she remembered to ask. But she never heard if her parents said yes or no, because she was already running.

"Sapphire! Sapphire!" Her voice rang out like a fire bell. Her trembling legs took her down, down past the walnut, toward the sycamores. She looked all around for her duck, tears blurring her vision. Then she blinked toward the water and saw the white spot, gliding, growing bigger. Then they were together, huddled against the patchy bark of the sycamore.

They sat for a long time. Lucy didn't say anything. A thick grey blanket of cloud rolled slowly in from the southwest and put out the sun. A cool breeze sprang up, rustling through the leaves and making Lucy shiver in her thin tank top.

"I don't know how to say good-bye to you, Saph," she finally decided, stroking her duck's wings. "I just don't know how to do it. I don't think I can." She closed her eyes, feeling the roughness of bark on her bare shoulders. Mother said to accept it. But she couldn't accept it. It was impossible. She just couldn't.

"We'll run away," she said, opening her eyes. But even as she said it, she knew it wouldn't work. It was hard enough to hide when you ran away by yourself. But when you had a duck with you...they'd find her in a minute.

She wondered, could she hide Sapphire in the park? Mom had said it was only two blocks away. But she knew there was no water there. And sometimes older boys brought slingshots in to hunt squirrels. The thought of it made her shudder. If anyone hurt Sapphire...

Suddenly Lucy picked up her head and listened. There was a slight crackling of twigs, a rustling, there, up on the hill. Someone or something was near. She turned and stood up, clutching Sapphire tightly, in case it was the Mayberrys' dog. But it was only Misty.

"Old Magic Misty," she said sarcastically. "Only this time I heard you coming. You must be slipping." She glared, as angry at herself as she was at the redheaded duck. She'd half believed in him. Half believed he was magic and that somehow he could save them. And look how it turned out.

Misty stood silently in the growing wind, seemingly unaware of her angry thoughts. He kept staring, not a feather ruffled, as if he were inside a glass bell jar. Lucy stared back, defiantly. She stared and stared at those golden eyes. She stared until they reminded her of coins again. She watched them multiply—two, four, a dozen coins, rising like bubbles from a pipe, then floating in black space. She blinked, trying to blink the vision away, but even when Misty was focused again and Lucy saw only golden eyes, the coins were still there, stacked like a single, nagging thought at the back of her mind. Why did he keep making her think of coins anyway? What good was it going to do now?

The rustling of twigs began again, only louder now. It was the bushes up and behind Misty that had been making the noise. Now the bushes waved violently. Parted in two. Something wooly and grey poked out.

"Oh!" Lucy exclaimed, stepping backward.

Out popped Mrs. Schrader's wild hair. Out popped Mrs. Schrader. She straightened up at once, but still looked like a grandmother wood elf, twigs and leaves scattered over her grey head.

"I didn't want you to see me coming," she said matter-of-factly, pulling a large maple leaf from behind her ear. "I thought you might run again. Hannah sent me."

"Oh," Lucy answered, setting Sapphire gently down, waiting for her to continue. But the old lady just stood like a flagpole, her thin brown dress flapping against her legs in the still-growing wind. She looked at Lucy, at Sapphire. She looked at Misty, who was practically at her feet.

"Well, what does he say?" she finally asked, pointing at the redhead.

"Misty? What difference does it make?" she asked bitterly. Just the same, it seemed he flashed gold inside her mind again, gold that lit her dark heart like fireflies.

"No, Lucy. Not Misty. Bluebill. If it is Bluebill. And if it is," she said harshly, "it'll do more good to ask him what to do that it will to cry."

Lucy looked at the ground, angry at Mrs. Schrader for thinking her a cry baby. How would she like it if she were going to lose *her* duck? But in spite of herself, her eyes snuck a glance at the blue-billed duck. And then Mrs. Schrader was going on again. She'd forgotten all about scolding Lucy. Her voice was whispery and urgent.

"Don't you see, Lucy? If it is Bluebill, he's obviously here to help. He didn't come until Mrs. Rummel decided to sell the house, did he?"

"No," said Lucy, looking up at Mrs. Schrader.

"He said he'd come to help, didn't he?"

Lucy considered. "Yes," she said quietly. That was what he'd seemed to be saying.

"Well then, what does he say now, Lucy?"

Lucy wavered. She wanted to believe. She did. But what if she just wanted him to be magic. "What if I just want him to be magic?" she asked out loud. "What if I just think he's saying things at me. He's never told me where to look. He's never said one specific thing. What if he's really just a mixed-up redhead who flew South too soon? The Dourmans are coming on Thursday, Mrs. Schrader! What if I'm just imagining things I want to hear? I've got to think about Sapphire now—not Misty!"

"Pish-tosh. You listen to me, young lady," snapped Mrs. Schrader, pointing her bony finger at Sapphire, "I'd take that duck home myself—all the way to Scranton— before I'd see the likes of the Dourmans come near her. And I've got a pond. And I love ducks. So stop letting your worry about Sapphire keep you from thinking straight."

Lucy blinked in surprise, beginning to protest that Sapphire was too shy, but Sapphire had already begun walking over to Mrs. Schrader, who bent down and scooped her up as if she were somebody's pet poodle. Sapphire didn't squawk or wave her wings in alarm. She didn't wiggle or jerk.

"Besides," Mrs. Schrader added, "the reason Hannah sent me out was to tell you she'd take Sapphire, if you want. Of course, Hannah doesn't know beans about ducks. Half the time she forgets to feed Blackie. But of course if Hannah takes her, you could visit. Now," she said briskly, "let's get back to the subject of Misty."

Lucy looked at Mrs. Schrader, who was stepping down, around, staring at the still silent duck. She was obviously trying to get a message herself. In her brown dress, she looked like a tree.

Lucy shook her head in amazement. Two solutions for Sapphire. Just like that. Of course, they weren't as good as keeping Sapphire, but anything was better than leaving her to the Dourmans. And now... What if she did give Misty a chance? Could she, did she dare hope there might be a chance at an even better solution?

"Mrs. Schrader?" she interrupted. "You know, the duck keeps making me think of gold coins. Once I thought I even saw them on the grass. And come to think of it, that very first time, I was thinking of coins when it was raining onto the creek..."

"Wonderful!" boomed Mrs. Schrader, turning back to Lucy. "Now we're getting somewhere. I knew that duck was magic."

Lucy frowned. "But what good is it to tell me there are coins? I already know that. I need to know where. And I need to know right away."

Mrs. Schrader frowned back at Lucy. "Child, it's up to you, too, you know. A seed won't grow till you put it in soil. A duck can't swim except in water. And magic only works in an atmosphere of belief. Do you believe, Lucy?"

Lucy blinked in surprise. "Hadn't Misty asked that—if she believed?"

"Do you believe all the way, Lucy?" Mrs. Schrader continued, "in spite of what people around you think or how late it's getting? Which reminds me," she added, looking up at the darkening sky. "We'd best be getting back."

"Sometimes I believed," Lucy thought, as they made their way up against the wind. "But then I doubted again.

Is that something you can help? Can you make yourself believe more than you do?" She shook her head, thinking somehow it didn't make sense to choose a belief, because your mind kept going the way it went, no matter what. Still, for Sapphire, anything was worth a try. Her heart beat a little faster, as she thought of keeping her pet duck. She would shoo every doubt away. She hoped.

"Remember too," added Mrs. Schrader as they pushed open the back door, "Magic comes in its own time—like a flower blooming. You can't rush it. And Lucy—you've got to do your part. Don't forget what I told you."

CHAPTER THIRTEEN

A GIFT FOR LUCY

Mom had left the drapes open in the living room, and from inside, the dusk looked like night. Some of the windows were open, to cool the house, but others looked like black mirrors, reflecting lamplight and relaxed faces. Mom had made coffee and put out butter mints and the box of chocolates Mrs. Phillip had given her for being so patient with her cat.

"Would you like one?" Mom asked, lifting the box toward her as she entered the room.

Lucy took a piece and headed for the empty couch cushion where Mrs. Rummel was drumming her wrinkled hand.

"I saved you a spot," she said smiling.

"Thank you about Sapphire," Lucy said.

"Hannah's been telling us all about life in the farmhouse back in the twenties and thirties," said Dad, leaning back in the easy chair.

"Yeah," said Nick, who was next to the coffee table, dipping into the butter mints. "Remember that hole in the wall we found when we first moved in? It was from a woodstove connected to the summer kitchen fireplace."

"And there was a pump for the well by the back gate," added Winnie.

"Neat!" was all Lucy could managed. Her mouth was full of maple cream. After she swallowed she added, "They're fun!"

Mrs. Rummel laughed. "Elva and I certainly never thought so. When we stayed with Gram it was our chore to get water for cooking and washing clothes. On washdays we'd be so tired we'd never even play after supper, but go right to sleep."

"Where did you sleep?" asked Winnie, who was sitting on the other side of Mrs. Rummel

"In the little room facing the creek."

"My room!" said Lucy, pleased. "Mrs. Rummel slept in that pretty bed up in the attic, didn't you Mrs. Rummel?"

The old lady nodded.

"The bed's exquisite," said Mom. "I've often admired it. We'll have to be sure it's returned to you, along with the other Rummel things, when we leave next month."

Lucy squirmed in her seat. She hated the way Mom made it sound so certain. But Mrs. Rummel touched her hand then. She looked up.

"I...I was thinking of that bed before I came tonight—where I should put it, how I would use it. Lucy," she said, turning, "I want you to have it."

Lucy was so surprised that for a minute she didn't say anything. "That lovely old bed. For me?"

"Yes, Lucy, my friend"—and at these words she smiled and her blue eyes went watery—"for you. I couldn't give you the farmhouse, although I wanted to very much. But what I can give you I will. Take it. Have lovely dreams in it. And give it to your own little girl one day."

"Thank you. Oh thank you," Lucy said, throwing her arms around the old lady. "I just love you," she whispered, so only Mrs. Rummel could hear.

"I know," Mrs. Rummel whispered back. "I love you too."

♋ ♋ ♋

The rest of the evening passed quickly. They introduced the old ladies to Clue, and Mrs. Schrader took to the game immediately, playing with intense concentration and skill. Dad made popcorn on the third round, but Lucy and Mrs. Rummel bowed out for a final tour of the house before she had to leave. It was slow going because of the walker and Lucy having to keep turning lights out so Mrs. Rummel could see through the windows. Her favorite view was from the front door, which faced the hill.

"Best of all I loved this tree," she said.

They stood on the dark doorstep and looked at it. Funny, Lucy thought, how on a clear night the sky looked almost blue-black, but on a cloudy one it looked light. The huge walnut rose up before them, and silhouetted against the clouds, it looked like a giant.

"Why, it must be well over 100 years old. Gran said it was here even when she was a girl, though it was small then. Isn't it grand?"

The rest of the family found them there, in the hallway. Mrs. Schrader was carrying two pocketbooks and Mrs. Rummel's shawl too.

"Goodbye, dear Lucy," Mrs. Rummel said as she turned around in a flutter of moths by the back door. "Sleep well."

"How can I help it in that wonderful bed?" Lucy answered.

"Watch Bluebill closely, Lucy. And listen," whispered Mrs. Schrader, just before she turned and walked away.

"I will," Lucy called back.

Then the two old ladies disappeared into the backseat, and Mother into the front, and then the car was gone.

"I ought to have my head examined for promising to set this bed up tonight," her Dad said, opening the door to the cellar where he kept his tools.

"Thanks, Dad," Lucy called down to him.

"Run up to the attic with a dust rag," he yelled up to her. "I'll take your own bed apart first."

Lucy got a flashlight, some dust rags and furniture polish, then stepped back into the living room for the rest of the popcorn. She left that in her room for Dad before heading up the attic stairs.

The wind whistled eerily up there, sending gusts of cool air across the floor. Lucy worked quietly in the dim light. She started with the big headboard, which had three sunken panels: two little ones and a big one. The middle was a rectangle that held a circle of flying birds and flowers. The two smaller panels were squares, each with one bird facing the middle. She was carefully polishing one of them out of its blanket of dust when Nick came up.

"Well," he said, shaking his head bleakly, "I guess my termite plan wasn't so hot."

"I know," she said smiling up at him. "But I think there still might be hope." She handed him a rag and told him what Mrs. Schrader said about Bluebill coming back and the gold coins and what she said about ghosts. And about magic.

Nick listened intently, as if he were Lucy, listening to Mrs. Schrader for the first time, out in the windy dusk. "I don't know," he finally said. "When I first touched Misty I thought—'This is no ghost.' But remember that story of the hitchhiker on the road that got in the car and then disappeared? I mean, didn't he open the car door? He must have been solid to do that. And he fooled the driver, after all. Maybe Misty is a ghost." He threw his head back and laughed. "Whoa! What if he really is! You're right, Lu. We've got to keep watching him." Then he frowned. "I just hope Misty's not in one of his disappearing moods tomorrow."

"He's got to be around," Lucy countered. "I mean, if he's come to help, he has to be, right? And he has come to help," she added firmly. "So I'm sure we'll see him."

But was she so sure? Even when she finally fell into her freshly polished, newly sheeted bed, she was still wondering. Was she sure? But the wind soon drowned out thoughts of the blue-billed duck and the treasure and old beds and everything else.

♋   ♋   ♋

The next thing Lucy knew there was a blue bird sitting on her window ledge. She blinked her eyes in the bright sunshine, surprised last night's clouds hadn't turned to rain, surprised that the screen was missing from her window. Had it blown off the night before?

Lucy smiled, delighted to have a bird half inside her own room. The thought occurred to her that he looked like the bird carved on her new bed and she remembered what Mrs. Rummel said about the bed being magic and the birds coming alive. She sat up quietly, determined to get close, but the bird seemed to sense her thoughts and turned and flew away.

Lucy ran to the window. Maybe he had a nest nearby and she could see where it was. She raised the window a little higher and peered out.

"Oh!" she cried out in surprise. She stepped back, unbelieving, and feeling a little light-headed, she grabbed onto the window ledge. She closed her eyes and opened them again. She did it again. And again. But what Lucy saw was always the same. And what Lucy saw was astonishing.

CHAPTER FOURTEEN

THE KEY

The walnut tree had disappeared! And the beeches! The hill was bare. No mounds of ivy nor daylily, no great thrusting branches, no sun-glittery canopy of green. Just a slender young tree, standing alone on a great expanse of empty hillside.

It was so small and faraway, Lucy could barely make out the shape of its leaves. She bent forward, squinting, and saw stems with pointed leaflets, paired side by side. And there—there were a pair of yellow-green husks. So it was a walnut too—but so small!

She turned her gaze now toward the other trees and gasped. Because beyond the sparse group of young saplings was the old road! It was dirt and followed the stream, curving like a brown snake between trees she'd never seen before, tall sycamores and honey locusts that rose skyward from the foot of the forested hill that once held a flat grey highway.

Lucy's heart was thumping hard. What magic was happening to her? What was happening? Her knees went trembly when she reached for her robe. It was there, hanging from the row of pegs where she'd left it. But next to it was a blue-checked dress, long, with a ruffle at the bottom. A white bonnet had been placed over the top of it. Underneath, next to Lucy's red thongs, were a pair of black shoes with golden buckles. She turned toward the opposite wall, toward her desk and the stack of library books and her half-eaten licorice bar. But all she saw was a pine table with an inkwell, a candle in a brass holder, three brightly colored stones and a bunch of wood violets that hadn't been put in water and were getting limp.

Lucy left the room on legs of jelly, hesitating at the top of the stairs where white-washed walls had replaced papered ones. Everything seemed curiously light. Was it because of the walls? Then Lucy remembered. The tall trees were gone. There were no leaves to filter the sunlight.

Downstairs, the hall looked different—wider, in spite of the sitting bench and little tables holding vases of daisies. On the floor was a braided rug, which she stepped onto quietly, thinking how springy and new it felt.

The kitchen door was gone and Lucy ran to the dining room to see why. She peeked inside an enormous room—two rooms combined. The fireplace was in the middle of them now, only it didn't look at all familiar. The hearth was bigger, for one thing, with room enough for hanging pots. There were pots on the outside too. One was half as big as a bathtub and shiny as a new penny. Lucy knew it was an apple butter pot because Mrs. Rinehart collected antiques and had one. The table in this room was where the Petersons had theirs, only it was pine, and the chair backs had heart cut-outs.

On the far side of the room, in the old kitchen part, was a tall pie safe with punched tin doors. Next to it on the floor was a butter churn and assorted crocks. A blue cupboard was where their sink used to be. Dirty dishes were stacked to one side, and on the bottom shelf were water buckets. She couldn't tell for sure what was on the back wall without going past the china cabinet on her left, and she didn't dare do that, for now she heard a noise in the kitchen, a kind of muffled thump—thump—thump.

"Patches! I should thrash you!"

Lucy nearly jumped out of her skin. She turned quickly back into the hallway. Luckily, the lady had only raised a floured hand and retreated. She was young and slender and wore a white apron over a long dress with the same blue checks Lucy had seen upstairs. Her hair was pulled back under a white cap, but a few dark wisps had escaped, falling in ringlets around her red-cheeked face. Luckily her eyes had been on the cat she was chasing and not on the doorway.

The rust and white and grey and black kitten was curling around Lucy's legs now. Its whiskers and its small pink nose were dusted lightly with flour, and it looked up at her with eyes of lightest, purest blue. Lucy longed to pick it up, but knew she mustn't. She had to get out of the house. What if the lady saw her? What would she say?

She pulled the heavy front door back hoping against hope it wouldn't squeak as it usually did. Surprisingly, it opened easily, gliding without a sound.

How strange everything looked out here. How sunny and open! Lucy walked down the bare hill. She wanted a better look at the road.

From up close she could see it was narrow, barely wide enough for one car and full of ruts and holes and rumpled, bindweed. She stood in the center of it and looked back at the house. It seemed impossible. Could this really be her house? With the newish wooden wing gone, it looked straight and boxlike. In the sun, it was bright-looking too, despite those strange dark-blue shutters. There it was, sitting in a world as foreign as Mars, the once familiar southwest highway lost to forest. And behind the house was the biggest surprise of all.

There it stood. As big as the Carlisle Courthouse. As big as the Mount Holly Inn. It was a grand barn, dark red wood on the top and grey ledgestone, like the house, on the bottom, except where the white double doors were.

She ran back toward it now. As she approached she smelled the sharp clean smell of animals and heard the lowing of cows. Lucy examined the stone work from close up. The pieces were laid together just so, just like the house. She reached out a hand. It was scratchy and cool. And real.

It's so big! she thought. It must reach clear back to the frog pond. How ever could they build a barn on that? She thought of the mucky land on toward the meadow, of how it flooded so badly after spring rains that she and Nick would float the inflatable raft there, and later in the season, when the water was gone, search for frogs or wild ducks' nests filled with large greenish eggs. She ran to see, half expecting dark water grasses to be stretching away right from its back door. But coming around the corner she saw that she'd misjudged the distance. The water grasses were further out. Or had they moved? Everything looked so different. The whole marsh seemed to have shrunk, the rushes and blue flag and sedge congealed into a dark curving line which began far, far away and traveled, growing lighter, then lighter, then lighter still, disappearing about fifteen yards from her feet. The only thing that broke the snake-like line was the small building that sat atop it just a few feet from the back of the barn. "The springhouse!" she thought.

She ran closer and heard the trickling, the clear sound of running water. And then another sound, a wonderful, familiar sound. It was someone she knew! She'd recognize that quiet, high-pitched quacking anywhere. Misty! Of course it was Misty—or perhaps she should call him Bluebill here—here in the past where he came from.

He was sitting just to one side of the doorway, quacking his head off at her.

The duck approached as she did, coming out from the overhanging roof into the sunshine. Something was glinting on his chest, something silver, something that bounced as he waddled toward her.

Lucy was staring so hard that she forgot to say hello. Instead she only whispered, "What are you wearing?" even though she could plainly see that it was a small silver key that dangled from a chain around Misty's neck.

As she knelt down in front of him, Misty tipped his reddish head and the chain fell off and landed in Lucy's lap.

Lucy picked up the key. The top of it was shaped like a heart and the narrow tip had two tiny prongs. It was as small as a pencil eraser, small enough to fit inside a jewelweed blossom. She pressed her hand around it hard and looked at Misty. "Thanks, Misty. I mean, Misty Bluebill," she added with a smile.

He answered in a Misty-way, the thought coming loud and clear: "Find the treasure. Find the treasure now, Lucy."

Lucy held tight to the key and shut her eyes, willing to hear more. To hear where. She saw bright coins again, but they weren't in a place. All she saw was deep blackness. "Where? Where do I look?" she asked, opening her eyes again and searching Misty's own.

But the duck just stared back—silently. Lucy shut her eyes again, trying desperately to get a picture, listening for an answer. She felt the hardness of the key in her palm. "What does this belong to?" she wondered.

But no picture came. No words. Only a loud banging.

Lucy opened her eyes.

"C'mon, Luce, it's almost 9:30. Are you getting up or not?"

"Huh?" Lucy said, rubbing her eyes, then looking blankly up at the old, familiar light bulb on her ceiling.

"Lu, are you all right?"

Lucy sat up, looked around her room—at her messy desk, her yellow robe on its peg, the denim shorts next to them, the jeans next to them... She looked down at her hand, still clenched tight. She uncurled it slowly, still expecting to see the key. But it was empty. All she saw were the marks from her own fingernails.

But it had been so real!

"Lucy!" Nick sounded exasperated.

"I'm up," she finally said in a quiet voice. "Come on in."

It had begun to rain sometime during the night. Now, when Lucy told her story she was accompanied by the slow, steady sound of drizzle. Occasionally the wind would come up and send heavy sprays against her window.

Mother looked astounded when they came down to breakfast in waders. She smiled a puzzled smile, then suggested they wait for the sun before going out to fish.

"We're not going out to fish," Lucy said.

"Lucy had a dream last night," Nick added in explanation.

Winnie, who'd studied dreams in her high school psychology class, left her cinnamon roll dough in the kitchen.

"Mrs. Wilson said once in a while people dream things that come true," she said, sitting down across from Lucy. It wasn't about the treasure, was it?"

Lucy smiled excitedly, then told it over again. "I think it's a sign, Winnie. I think there's something by the old springhouse."

"Whoa!" Winnie said excitedly. "I'll come out to look too—right after my dance lesson."

Mother had also been listening. She was leaning against the wall by the fireplace, warming her hands on her coffee cup. She opened her eyes now, shaking her head, scrunching up her forehead.

"Lucy there isn't a thing in that dream that would make it in any way extraordinary. It was about things you already know—that Misty looks like Bluebill, who's from the past. That Mr. Wickfield thought the springhouse held a clue."

"But the key..." Lucy protested.

"And I'm surprised at you, Winnie. Getting Lucy all worked up when you ought to know better. Didn't your teacher tell you that dreams are made of symbols. Tell her what a key is."

Winnie frowned. "A key could be a symbol for something you want to find or find out about," she said reluctantly. "But Mom," she added, "Lucy's dream was very vivid. And vivid dreams are usually the ones that come true. Some dreams do come true. Don't you remember that *Real Life Mysteries* show about the guy who dreamed he was going to have an accident, and then he found himself on that same road he dreamed about and saw that same car..."

Mom rolled her eyes. People have clairvoyant dreams once or twice in a lifetime. If at all. And I always thought it happened more to sensitives, people who have ESP."

"But you always say Lucy has ESP with animals," Nick reminded her. "And Misty's an animal, isn't he?"

Mom rolled her eyes. She forced a laugh "It was a joke...." She stopped as she met Lucy's eyes.

"Sometimes I think Lucy does have ESP, Mom, don't you?" But no one was listening to Winnie, because Lucy was interrupting, talking twice as loud.

"You promised Mom. You promised I could tell you things, and you wouldn't make fun. And that you'd be on my side. You'd help."

"Yes, I promised," Mom said, coming over to set her cup down. "I haven't forgotten. It's just that I need to give you my opinion on this and ask that you consider it. I'm not going to stop you from looking." She glanced at her watch. "I'll even help..."

The kids broke out in cheers "but I need to make sure you remember your side of the promise. Let me hear you say that on Thursday, when the papers are signed, you'll help the rest of us by accepting reality and try to be happy in spite of all this."

Lucy nodded, not wanting to remember that Thursday was the day after tomorrow.

While Mom changed her clothes, Lucy and Nick looked for Misty—in case he had some clues to give. But they couldn't find him anywhere, and then Mom was on the porch, pulling on her boots, so the three of them headed for the meadow.

In the back of the vanished barn, in the middle of a coolish drizzle, Lucy looked around. How far from the barn had the springhouse been? And the marsh grass was all over the place this morning. If the dream had been real, then a century could sure change things.

Mother was getting impatient. Her forehead was all scrunched. She was biting her lip while she kicked at the weeds. But out loud she only complained about a leak in her left boot.

"Just start anywhere," Nick whispered. "We can move later if you figure it out."

So Lucy picked a spot. A gurgly, mushy spot that very well might be the place, for all she knew. Everyone looked relieved and began digging at once, Mom with the short spade, Lucy and Nick with hand trowels.

It was nice that the wet earth gave so easily under the blades, but the bottoms of the holes filled with water so they had to look blind, dipping in and feeling for anything hard and not shaped like stones.

They worked quite happily for an hour or so, ignoring their cold, wrinkling fingers, talking about Mrs. Phillip's cat and how he wouldn't sit still to be painted and kept coming over to drink Mom's brush water, then about Mrs. Schrader's skill in Clue, and then what they should do with those old pennies they'd found with the metal detector. Mom said Mrs. Schrader's husband was a numismatist, which meant he bought and sold old coins. So maybe she could take them home with her to see if they'd be worth anything.

After a while they started to take breaks. Nick and Lucy used theirs to look for Misty, but they didn't see him anywhere. As the morning wore on, they stood up and stretched more and more often and laughed less and less.

By noon the rain had begun again. It was coming down lightly but steadily. Mom had gone to the college to see Professor Dawson about an art class she'd be teaching, but before she left she said she'd start some soup.

Now Nick reminded Lucy about eating. "I'm starving, aren't you? Let's go in. For just a few minutes. We can come right back out."

"Go ahead," Lucy told him. "I'll be right there. Honest," she added, seeing him hesitate.

Then she was alone. Except for Sapphire, who'd come to keep her company, nosing happily in the water. She looked white and bright and happy to be surrounded by dozens of puddles. Lucy sighed. Wouldn't it be nice to be a duck. Her back was getting a kink.

"Here, squirt," a voice interrupted. It was Winnie, dressed in waders and Mom's slicker. She had a trowel in one hand and a steaming cup in the other. "Mom made me promise not to let you starve yourself or drown in one of those puddles you're digging."

"Thanks, Winnie," Lucy said, reaching up for the thermos cup. It was warm and felt good on her hands, except for the place below her thumb where the blister was coming. She walked with it toward the meadow swing, swiped at the water on the plastic seat, then sat down. The tomato soup was wonderful, warming her through. How nice it was to sit down. How tired she was. It was as if she hadn't slept at all the night before. Her dream had been hard work. And all this was even harder.

When Mother came home at 3:00 she couldn't believe they were all still out there and marched everybody back to the house for a break. "Thirty minutes at least, understand?" Then she muttered something under her breath about pneumonia and the whole thing was preposterous.

No one complained very much, especially when they saw the coconut washboard cookies and the cream-filled chocolate bars she'd brought home. Lucy sat down on the oak rocker after her tea. The grey of the day, the soft patter of the rain, and the soothing motion of the chair made her feel drowsy, and soon she dozed off in spite of herself.

When she woke up it was pouring, and Mother absolutely forbade opening the back door until it let up. So she and Nick went over her dream again, step by step, searching the dream instead of the mud for answers. Lucy rocked and Nick paced.

He stopped in front of the picture window, and turned to Lucy. "The way I see it, if your dream wasn't just a wish, like Mom says, then there are just two important things in it."

"I know," Lucy replied. "The springhouse and Misty."

"Right. And we can take care of the springhouse OK by ourselves. But what about Misty? Where's he been all day anyway?" He turned back and peered out, down toward the creek, which was high and murky and running fast.

Lucy thought again about Mrs. Schrader and how she'd said to listen to Misty. How was she supposed to do that when she couldn't even find him? She frowned. "You know him. He only appears when he wants to."

"I wish I knew where he lives. Where he sleeps."

"Me too. But maybe he lives in some kind of spirit world or something and only comes here when he wants to."

Nick looked toward the doorway, then Lucy did too. It was the kind of statement that would worry Mom. But they both knew it might be true."

After supper the rain stopped, although water was still dripping from the trees, dimpling the stream and all the fresh puddles in the squidgy, saturated earth. As the three children marched back toward the meadow, the sun found a chink in the clouds and broke through in long golden rays, making them feel hopeful again.

They fell to digging at once, knowing nightfall was coming. It was horrible work, much wetter than before. Nick joked about renting diving gear and goggles. Winnie went back to the house for tissues, for hot chocolate, for a phone call. But she always came back. She was a pretty good big sister, after all, even if she did call Lucy a squirt.

Two hours passed. The clouds were moving. Half the sky cleared, showing a silver moon. The air was growing purpley and cold.

"Lucy, there's still tomorrow," Winnie finally said softly.

In the distance they heard the porch bell—their signal to come home.

"You go ahead," said Lucy. "Tell Mom Nick and I will be right there. I'm just going to try this one last spot. Maybe this was the springhouse. Maybe this hard thing down here was part of the foundation."

Winnie looked exasperated. She turned to Nick for support.

"We will be in. Tell Mom five more minutes, OK?"

"She's going to turn me right around to come back for you," Winnie said. "OK. I'll walk slow." And with that she turned to go and nearly fell flat on her face, tripping over a small grey mound just behind her.

"Oh, rats!" she cried, pulling her hands out of the mud. She swiped at her face with her sleeve, and winced at the cold wetness. She glared at the duck.

Misty only looked at her calmly, then continued on, toward Lucy and Nick and the biggest, splashiest puddle.

"Where was he all day when we needed him?" Winnie snapped. "Where was the great red-headed mystery solver when we were working our tails off and getting sopping wet to boot?" And she turned to go again but stopped once to look back. And just in time.

Misty was through with the puddle now. He shook himself off as if to say, enough of fun, and now to work. Then he walked straight to a smaller puddle, quite close to where Lucy was and began nosing around in earnest. Then his tail feathers began wagging and his head began to shake back and forth then up and down, as if he were pulling at something. Winnie came closer and put her trowel down.

Lucy watched, amazed, as he stuck his whole red head into the water. When it came up there was a dark, slimy string hanging from his beak.

"What is it?" whispered Nick.

Lucy inched over. And just as if she were back inside her dream, Misty came to her, dipped his head and dropped the chain into her lap. For it was a chain. She felt the small, delicate links under her fingers as she skimmed the mud off. She held it up now toward Nick and Winnie so they could see and rubbed the mud from the object that dangled at the end of the dirty, wonderful loop. It was badly tarnished. It was black and green. But it was a key. Heartshaped, with two tiny prongs.

CHAPTER FIFTEEN

LOVE--AND A QUESTION

"The key! It's the key! It's the very one from my dream!"

"The key!" echoed Nick, throwing his trowel down, then ducking the muddy spray that flew up when it landed. He began to laugh, then to jump up and down, until he landed on an especially slippery patch and fell right into a puddle.

Winnie danced like a clumsy ballerina in her waders, twirling through the mud, face toward the moon, yelling, "It's ma-a-agic. Lucy's magic."

Lucy hugged Misty with one arm and reached for Nick with the other, trying to pull him up, but she slipped herself and fell into the puddle with him. Misty squawked a strange, high squawk they'd never head before and flapped his wings in alarm as he went down with Lucy.

Then all three children were splashing and laughing and slapping dirty sprays of water up into the cold night air where it caught the pearly light of moon before falling back again. They made so much noise they set the Mayberrys' dog howling and even brought Mom and Dad out to see.

Lucy's parents looked puzzled, as if they hadn't expected Lucy's dream to come true, or the keys to look so exactly alike, but mostly they made jokes about their children being able to do detergent commercials and finally headed everyone back in for showers and cocoa.

The children flopped into bed that night happy but exhausted. In their excitement they hadn't talked too much about the next step: finding whatever the key opened. Then it had seemed a mere detail. But in the morning, as they gathered around the dining room table, they began to realize it wasn't a detail at all.

"Did you dream anything last night?" Nick called hopefully from the kitchen as he popped two pieces of bread in the toaster.

Lucy stared into her raisin bran, trying to think if she'd dreamt anything at all the night before. She yelled back no.

Now Winnie was downstairs in her blue bathrobe asking Lucy the same question.

"No," she said again, feeling a little guilty as she looked into Winnie's crestfallen face.

"Well, in a way," Winnie said hesitantly as she sprinkled sugar on her cornflakes, "we're back where we started. We still don't have the faintest idea where the treasure is."

"Yeah," Nick added dejectedly. "But it's not really like being back where we started. Because now we only have one day left."

They considered this solemnly, but the ticking of the dining room clock nudged them into conversation again.

"We've got to have a strategy," Nick said.

"We've got to find Misty first," answered Lucy.

"Right," agreed Winnie. "Maybe he'll lead us right to it, like he did with the key!" Her blue eyes sparkled with hope. For a second.

"Winnie, hon, I don't think that's going to happen."

It was Dad, listening from the kitchen. He came in with a coffee cup in his hand. He was frowning.

Mother followed. Lucy noticed that she had dark circles under her eyes, and that she was biting her lip.

"Dad and I have been discussing this," she began. "Did you dream anything last night, Lucy?"

Lucy looked down at her cereal. "No," she said, for the third time that morning.

Mom and Dad looked at each other, then back at Lucy.

"There! You see!" Mother said. "Lucy, you've just got to open your eyes and look at the truth."

"But my dream was true!" Lucy countered.

"Her dream was true!" echoed the others.

"That's right, Lucy," Mother continued. "You've had one special, come-true dream. And that's a real gift. Only not the kind you think. Not the gift of treasure or escape from the reality we're all in. No. You were given a tiny peek into the future. Your dream was a premonition—that you'd find a key and how you'd find it."

"Lucy, Lucy," her Dad said softly. "It was only a key. The key is all you'll probably find"

"But what about Misty?" Nick asked defiantly. "He's not a dream. And don't you think it's a little strange that he just appeared here out of nowhere and looks just like Mrs. Rummel's grandmother's duck and has the wrong feathers on and seems to be giving Lucy messages."

"Messages? What messages?" Dad looked alarmed.

Lucy felt her face go red. "I always felt he'd come to help. And when I looked at him, I'd think of gold coins...

Dad shoulders dropped. He sighed with relief and smiled. "Oh Lucy. Consider. My darling, has this ordinary red-headed duck given you one piece of information you didn't already have?"

Lucy tried not to consider. She had to have faith, the way Mrs. Schrader said. All the same, everything Misty said went parading right through her mind. He'd come to help. He'd come to help her with money. Coins. Did she believe? It wasn't much, was it? Still, there was something about him. Something extraordinary. There had to be!

"Look," Dad continued, running his fingers through his hair, "about this house. I just wanted to say...we both wanted to say...that we truly do wish we could keep you all here. We wish we had the money. But we don't. So Mom and I have looked hard for a place you'd really like. And we thought," he added, looking into his coffee cup, "that you'd understand and try to make the best of it."

Winnie patted Dad's shoulder. "We understand. We really do, Dad."

"You know, kids," Mom added, "the key to happiness isn't one you find buried in a meadow or buy in a store. It's inside you. Its in the way you look at things, how you appreciate all the blessings you already have. Can you understand that?"

They all nodded, but it didn't keep Lucy from asking, "Does this mean you don't want us to look today?" She looked at Mom, then at Dad, terrified they'd say yes.

Dad looked at Lucy and closed his eyes. When he opened them he glanced down at his watch. "A-OK rentals will be opening in ten minutes. Maybe I can just get there and be back before class." He turned in the doorway, toward three ecstatic faces, but his voice was sober.

"I don't want you to feel that you didn't give this treasure hunt your very best. Or didn't give magic a try. And who knows? Maybe Misty is magic. Who am I to say? But after tomorrow, I want your solemn word you will put this all behind you, and that you'll try to make the best of whatever comes next in our lives.

Of course they all promised. Lucy thought it was especially nice that Dad had said that about magic, because

126

she knew inside that not in a million years, would her dad believe in magic. Not if it dropped on his head.

While Dad went back for another detector, Lucy and Nick looked for Misty. They searched up and down the creek, all over the rose-covered hill, inside the shallows, on the pond, even up by the highway. Nothing.

"Why aren't you here when we need you the most?" Lucy thought uneasily.

"We can keep an eye out for him while we're working," Nick suggested. "After all, we've gone all over the house. All that's left is the outdoors anyway."

That was Dad's suggestion too. He said the springhouse site might be a good place to start. So after he sped away toward work, they headed for the meadow.

After the first hour or so, the day turned hot. It was muggy, too, and the low clouds that kept the sun out were keeping the gnats and horseflies in. One especially merciless one followed Lucy everywhere, in spite of her constant swatting and yelling, so even though she didn't find anything she was almost glad to go in for lunch, just to get away from it.

Afterward, Lucy went out to look for Misty one more time, but she soon gave up, pulling a piece of hot dog bun from her back pocket for Sapphire, who'd been waddling patiently after her.

"Maybe this is one of our last days together, so I don't care if I'm not supposed to feed you." Her voice was defiant, but inside she just felt scared—scared because tomorrow their house would belong to the Dourmans, because Sapphire would have to go away. Because nothing would ever be the same again.

She could almost feel the minutes, one by one, slipping away that afternoon as she pushed the machine over the springy grass. It made a lot of noise sometimes, but never, never for anything important. Every time it would go off, her heart would almost stop and she'd think, "This is it, we're saved." Then Nick would take the detector and she'd dig and dig, her heart pounding, and pull up a nail, a quarter, the top of a coffeepot.

By suppertime the meadow looked like it had been attacked by an army of moles. Mom looked at it frowning, but Nick said not to worry, the Dourmans were probably planning to pour concrete over it anyway.

"We're not going to leave it this way," Mom said sternly. "You kids are going to have to go right back out there tomorrow and pound the grass and weeds back into place."

Tomorrow. Could it really be coming? Without the treasure? That didn't seem possible. But already the detector was gone. Dad had come home early to get it back on time, returning a little later with big bags of fried chicken. Lucy barely touched her portion, excusing herself early so she could go back out and dig some more.

From the back door the green land fell away into the distance like an emerald sea. Twenty-five acres! And then she remembered what Mrs. Rummel had said about Elva's inheritance—all that land across the highway had been the Silverlings' too. What if the treasure were there?

"What's the use?" she thought, shrugging her shoulders and heading down by the creek. "I'll dig here—to be by Sapphire." It was as if everyone, finally, were thinking the same thing: they weren't going to find it. And now they were reaching out for comfort: Lucy to Sapphire, Nick to Lucy. Even Winnie came down for a while, to poke half-heartedly in the still damp earth and offer Lucy help in decorating her new room, "just in case they didn't find it." Mom and Dad were together too, walking slowly over the meadow, their heads down.

It grew dusky, and the mosquitoes came out. Then the moon. When it was finally dark and the stars were bright in the half of sky where the clouds had blown away, they all went quietly inside. The house seemed as still as the outdoors. Mom and Dad spoke in hushed tones. Winnie's radio stayed off. No one was interested in television.

Lucy, on Mom's insistence, took a shower and washed her hair, but afterwards asked to go out again for just five minutes to say good-night to Sapphire. She pulled on her old green sweater, let Mom tie a scarf around her still wet head, took the lantern and headed down toward the stream.

Everything looked eerie in the darkness, especially under the trees, and there was a high, funny wailing sound in the air. Lucy thought nervously of bats as she made her way down the hill. But near the water it was lighter and now she could see that it probably had been Misty. "Great time for you to show up," she thought silently. He was way, way up on the steepest part above the water. At least it looked like a copper-colored head glinting in the bushes. And the sound—that funny sound. She remembered now. It was how Misty had quacked when they found the key, and she'd pulled him into the puddle.

Sapphire was closer, curled under a jewelweed bush, and came quickly. Lucy sat for a long time just holding her. Stroking her. It was past five minutes, she knew. But she couldn't get up to go. She felt so uneasy. So puzzled.

Her mind was like the sky now—half one way and half another. She knew it was time to let go of her dream and start planning ahead. "Accepting reality," like Dad said. But somehow she couldn't quite do it. She'd believed in

Misty. Way down deep, when she wasn't just feeling sorry for herself, or worrying about things that might go wrong, or thinking what she ought to be thinking, she'd believed the funny redhead was magic. In a way, she guessed, she still did.

She looked up now, caught the red glint of feathers on the hill again. How could you explain Misty anyway? The way he'd come and go so fast. That he looked just like Bluebill. That he'd come in high summer dressed up for the cold. That he'd found the key. And most of all, that he told her things. Even if he'd hadn't told her the most important thing, he did talk to her.

It was all so confusing. And the worst was, grownups were never going to clear it up for her, because now she knew not all grownups agreed. Mrs. Schrader was grown up, wasn't she? And she faced the very same facts Dad did and didn't come out thinking like Dad at all.

Lucy bent and kissed the top of Sapphire's head. "What's real, huh, Saph? I love you. I know that. That's the realest of all. And I always will. No matter what. I heard them say it in church, Saph. 'Love never ends.' Nothing stops it. Not moving. Not the Dourmans. Not even dying."

Dying. Lucy looked up at Misty again. Misty, who was a ghost, after all, if you believed in him. He was closer, and she could see him better now out of the dark bushes and under the light of the stars. How beautiful he was!

Suddenly Lucy was thinking of the other Lucy—how she'd loved her own dear duck—and this land, this very spot, maybe—and her house and her Mom and her Dad. She felt it then: the love. It hadn't died at all, but was alive. It was real and all around her, pulsing like a heartbeat. She thought it was reaching out to her. To Lucy Peterson.

It was a matter of feeling it. Dad said you had to think things through, look at the facts, but Lucy realized there was more. Because people saw the same facts in different ways. In the end you had to listen to your feelings too. Sometimes they tell you things that thinking just can't. Like right now.

Right now she knew Lucy Silverling was still real and trying to reach out to her, to the other Lucy who loved ducks. That Bluebill was carrying the message on his own heart. Lucy looked up and looked solemnly at the duck on the hill. "I don't know why we couldn't find the treasure, Misty," she said out loud, looking the blue-billed duck straight in the eye. "I did my best. Honestly. And I do believe in you. And even though we didn't find it, I'm glad you came. I know you care about me."

Lucy gave Saph one last hug, set her down, then turned toward the house.

"How do birds fly, Lucy?"

Lucy spun around quickly. But already the red-headed duck had vanished. Only the words were left, ringing in her ears as clearly as if they'd been spoken aloud.

CHAPTER SIXTEEN

WINGS

Lucy sat in bed, leaning back on the tall headboard, ignoring what Mom said about wet hair not being good for old wood finishes. How could she lay down now? She was sure that Misty had just given her a very important clue, and she had to figure it out right now. The Dourmans would be in town in less than ten hours!

She hoped Nick was still up too. Between them, maybe they could figure it out in time. She listened, but there was no noise from his room, no steps in the hall. Just the steady tick-tick of her bedside clock.

She bit her lip and looked out the window. The sky was deep black, pierced with stars. One thin, high cloud drifted over the moon. "What a stupid question," she thought sleepily. "How do birds fly?" Misty should know better than I do. She pulled her covers up and felt sleep covering her too. A warm blanket of sleep. Her eyelids were closing all by themselves. "No!" she told herself, scooching up again, almost straight-backed against the headboard. She had to stay up until she figured out what Misty was trying to tell her. Before it was too late.

Was it something simple—like birds fly with wings? Wonderful. Where did that get you? Wings. Wings. Was the treasure in a bird's nest? Lucy forced herself to open her eyes wider, alarmed she could think anything so dumb. Birds' nests didn't last a hundred years. She must really be getting sleepy!

She remembered what Mrs. Schrader said about believing in magic before it could happen. Maybe flying was like that. That you had to believe before you could fly. Maybe that was the answer. Believing. So all you had to do was believe, and then you'd find the treasure. And that would be wonderful because then you could go to sleep because you were so tired.

No! No! You can't sleep. Lucy yawned. Slapped her own cheeks. Ran her fingers through her still-damp hair.

Wings. Wings. Soft, feathery wings. She closed her eyes, picturing Sapphire's small, shiny patches of blue. It would be so nice, she thought suddenly, if she were a baby bird, nestled under those soft, feathery wings. She shook her head. She shouldn't think of wings that way.

Maybe the treasure was buried under the new wing of the house. After all, it wasn't there in the first Lucy's time. But they could hardly dig that up by morning. She thought of the treasure there, hidden under the house, where it was dark. Dark and quiet. Dark and...

Lucy woke with a start. It was light outside. It was morning! "Oh, no!" she thought, wanting to jump right out of bed, but—"Ouch!" She'd slept sitting up, and a strand of her hair had gotten stuck on the headboard. Oooh. She rubbed her head where she'd felt it pull. She turned around. A few, glistening strands hung from the bottom of the small wooden bird's wing.

Lucy blinked. In that second she thought her heart stopped. She almost stopped breathing. The bird's wing! How could her hair have gotten stuck under that smooth carving anyway? She lifted a trembling hand, poked under the edge of the wooden wing with her fingernail. The bird's wing wasn't carved into the wood at all! It was glued on—very artfully. Her wet hair must have loosened the glue. She looked at it now, sticky and dark under her fingernail.

"Nick! Nick!" she cried out. She tried to jiggle the wing, to move it.

"Holy Guacamole!" yelled Nick from the doorway, understanding at once. "Hold it," he said, "I'll go get a screwdriver."

In another minute Winnie was there too, and they all watched breathlessly as the silver tip broke through the old glue. Then the wing was free, except at the very top, where it hung from a round wood pin.

Lucy pushed the wing tip and as it swirled up and around they heard a click, like a lock letting go. In back of the wing was a little indentation, just big enough for the tip of a finger. Lucy reached in and pressed down. Nothing happened. She jiggled her finger. There. It wanted to give toward the left. Why, the whole square that held the bird was a little sliding door. They pried under more glue, then pushed it back as far as it would go. Behind it, the thick wood of the bed had been carved out to hold a box the size of a cassette.

Lucy took it out with shaking hands and stared at the tiny metal lock.

"The key!" they all said at once. Lucy looked around frantically, not being able to think where it was. Winnie was already in her desk drawer, her sock drawer, her jewelry box.

"Calm down, Lucy," Nick said. "It's around your neck, remember?" But his own hands were shaking as he helped her get it off.

The fit was perfect. The tiny lock clicked. The key turned. The box opened. Lucy held it up, and the sun danced over golden coins.

"We found it! We found it!" Everyone was shouting at once. Lucy's eyes were full of tears, but she was laughing hard as Winnie spun her around, and Nick jumped up and down, and Mom and Dad raced up the stairs to see what the commotion was about.

"You what?" Mom asked, her eyes big as saucers.

"Whoa now," Dad said, "we better look at those coins before we decide they're really treasure."

Mom sat on the bed, working the little door over and over, shaking her head in astonishment as Dad inspected the coins, one by one. He tried to look stern as he spoke, but his eyes were shining.

"The face value of these coins doesn't amount to more than fifty dollars. Still," he added, "they might be rare, and they're in very good condition. We won't know for sure until we get in touch with John Schrader." He glanced at his watch. "We better get a hold of Hannah Rummel before she leaves to sign the sale papers."

"Spence," said Mom hesitantly, pressing on the small panel on the other side of Lucy's headboard, "I think this one was meant to open too... but it seems to be glued."

Lucy giggled. "You need to get it wet. Here," she said, handing her mom the key, "I'm going with Daddy to call."

Mrs. Rummel was so excited her voice was shaking. She said she'd postpone the morning meeting and tell Elva to call her husband and have him get back to Daddy right away.

While Lucy and Dad were pacing the kitchen floor waiting for the phone to ring, Nick and Winnie came racing down the stairs hooping and hollering and laughing. They plunked ten more coins down on the counter.

"Mom found them on the other side," Winnie explained.

It seemed like forever before Mr. Schrader called, although the wall clock told Lucy it had only been ten minutes. The children listened while Dad read the dates of each coin and the initials that told where they were minted. He repeated the one about the 1838 half dollar three times, then he smacked his forehead, and his face got red, and he twirled around and got tangled in the cord.

"What is it?" they whispered. He grabbed the phone pad, wrote "$40,000!" and held it toward them. Winnie barrelled back up the stairs to tell Mom while Lucy and Nick jumped up and down silently and whispered their hurrahs and hugged each other quietly.

When Dad got off the phone he said Mr. Schrader was driving in from Scranton to look the coins over and make sure, but he felt certain the half dollar alone could bring in as much as $40,000, and the others might bring several thousand more. When they called Mrs. Rummel back she could barely speak with all her laughing and crying. "Come tonight for supper, " Mom said gently. "You and John and Elva. We're going to celebrate!"

The rest of the day was dream-like: their running out to tell Saph, running back to tell Saph again, telling the chickens, looking for Misty, who was hiding out again, biking to Bixler's for peaches, checking to see if the coins were really there in the now-open boxes on the dining-room table. Lucy kept wondering if she'd wake up, like she had before, after her key dream.

But the afternoon came and went, and Lucy never woke up. And then it was 6:30, and here was Mrs. Rummel in the hallway in her violet-colored dress, eyes shining. And Mrs. Schrader, winking at her knowingly as she marched through the door. And Mr. Schrader, tall and blonde-grey and smiling.

"Yes," he told them, looking at each coin with a magnifying glass. "Very good condition," he announced. "They'll bring a handsome price."

When everyone went upstairs to see the bed, Lucy stayed behind with Mrs. Rummel, describing the hiding place carefully, so Mrs. Rummel wouldn't feel so bad about not being able to get up the stairs. She even told the rest of it—about Misty and the wing clue. She hadn't even told her parents that part yet. They'd thought it was an accident—just her hair getting stuck.

Mrs. Rummel touched that hair now, shaking her head, her eyes bright as candles. "It's all so... so miraculous, isn't it?" she asked. "Who knows?" she added. "After all, my grandmother used to tell Elva and me that Misty came back for her wedding, and that he flew three times around..."

Just then they heard the family on the stairs. Mrs. Schrader was saying it was a perfect hiding place, even without the glue, that maybe Mr. Silverling had added that as an extra precaution when the Confederate Army was coming close. That and perhaps moving the key out of the house. "In any case," she added, "it was an incredibly clever hiding place."

"No wonder no one's found it all these years." That was Mr. Schrader's voice. "Desks with fake-bottomed drawers, secret cupboards, panels, passageways. I've heard of them all. But beds—never!"

Mom laughed. "Well, I did. Once, in a college history class. Did you know there was a french army general who carried his money around in a folding bed? Of course, I never thought of that when we were looking. We even moved the bed carefully out of the way when we were using the detector."

That made her mother laugh. Then Dad joined in. Pretty soon, everyone was laughing.

Dinner was wonderful: steak and mashed potatoes, Lucy's favorite. And for dessert, fresh peaches and vanilla ice cream. Afterwards they sat in the living room. Dad and Nick opened all the windows because it was so warm in the house, while Lucy settled herself next to Mrs. Rummel and watched Mom pour iced tea. Winnie went around with a dish of mints.

"Well, Hannah," Dad said, "What are you going to do with all that money, besides paying your practical nurse and hanging on to this house for a while making us the happiest tenants in the world?"

"Oh, but I'm not going to hang on to it at all. I'm still going to sell it."

Lucy looked up in alarm. Mrs. Rummel was smiling mischievously. "I have a very special family in mind," she added.

"But we don't have any money..." Lucy began.

"Lucy," Mrs. Rummel said seriously, "my family has been looking for that money for a long, long time. You deserve a reward for finding it. Elva and John and I have decided that reward should be something substantial. We were thinking of, say, enough for a sizable down payment on a charming, two-hundred-year-old farmhouse. When you put enough down, you know, your payments wouldn't have to be very high—not higher than what you're paying for rent, I bet."

"You mean it would be ours? Our very own?"

"Exactly," she said. "And then you'd never have to leave. Not unless you wanted to. So if your parents think it's all right..."

Lucy looked at her parents. For a moment they were speechless. Then Mom's face got all red and she started laughing. "Pinch me, Spence, I think I've died and gone to heaven."

Then everyone laughed, and Dad said seriously "Are you sure, Mrs. Rummel? You know we love this place— but it's been in your family for years."

"I'm sure," Mrs. Rummel replied. "If I left it to my son, I know he would just sell it. His heart's in the West now. And Elva has no children. No, I feel you are the right family for this house. Lucy and Nick seem like my own grandchildren." She looked at them and added happily, "And now you won't have to say goodbye to any of those animal friends of yours. Not ever."

"Oh!" The word escaped from Lucy's lips, and she stood up suddenly. "But I think I do. Excuse me for a minute." And without waiting for her parents' reply, she ran out the door, down the hall, and outside.

It was Misty, of course, that Mrs. Rummel had reminded her of. And then, at that very moment came the thought, swift and strong: he was leaving. And he wanted to say goodbye.

Outside the air was perfectly still. The only wind was the one she made for herself running down the hill. She sky had finally cleared completely, and the reflected light of the moon made the creek look like a white satin ribbon. But there was no moving spot swimming on the water, no noise of squawking, only the trickling sound of the moving creek.

Well, he wasn't on the water, but she would find him this time. She knew it. He wanted her. And that made all the difference.

She looked back up the hill. The family was coming outside too. Dad was opening lawn chairs. Mom was stirring another pitcher of something. She could hear the faint sound of clinking ice and low laughter.

Lucy turned back and headed toward the bushes. She wished she'd brought her flashlight. She was about to step into the tangle of wild rose when Sapphire poked at her foot and made her jump.

"Oh, Sapphire," she said breathlessly, her heart pounding faster as she scooped her up and kissed her. "You're so much nicer to see than a garter snake."

Lucy turned then, peering in all directions. The feeling was so strong. So urgent. She stopped, closed her eyes to concentrate better. There was a message of some sort trying to come through. It was coming like waves, though she couldn't read it yet. It was pounding inside her head. It was like the beating of a heart, like the beating of wings. Wings!

Lucy looked up. The sky was dark and glittery. The Milky Way was pouring stars in a white stream over the top of the sky, over the top of the house. And there! There he was! He was flying over the house. He was going—yes, he was going to go around the chimney!

"Bluebill!" she called out loud. "Misty! Bluebill!" she called again, walking fast, running up the hill, Sapphire bouncing in her arms.

The family looked down at Lucy, then up at the sky.

Once, twice, he flew through the starry sky, swooping down and around the chimney. Lucy came to a stop at the top of the hill, right where Mrs. Rummel in her lawn chair was whispering into the sky: "So Gran's magic was real after all."

"Goodbye Bluebill," Lucy said quietly, knowing she didn't need to yell now. He was listening. "Thank you. And tell the other Lucy thank you, too."

The third time the duck swooped down to make his curve round the chimney, Lucy thought he looked down and right at her. Then, giving that high-pitched squawk that this time meant good-bye, he turned and headed into the night sky, not straight and low as ducks usually do, but up, up, higher and higher, until he was just another tiny, vibrant speck in a dark sea of stars.

"And thank you too," she added, finally taking her eyes off the sky to look at Mrs. Rummel. Then they both started to laugh, out of sheer happiness.

"Now how in the world did he learn to do that?" said Dad, still looking up, scratching his head.

"Magic... Magic... Magic..." The answer came from Nick as he slowly turned three perfect cartwheels on the grass, surrounded by his chickens, all except for Lips, who had flown onto Elva Schrader's arm when she'd first lifted it, to point toward the wings of the ghost in the star-filled sky.

The End